CALCULATED RISK

About the Author

Ever since her first climb, on a camping trip in Joshua Tree, Katherine Rupley has enjoyed the thrill and contentment that comes from scaling walls outside and inside. She has done bouldering, top rope, and traditional lead climbing.

Katherine is also an avid reader, runner, traveler, and photographer. She's always up for a hike or a travel adventure in search of another new experience or skill to learn. She lives in Los Angeles with her wife and their three spoiled cats (all rescues).

www.KatherineRupley.com
@KatherineRupleyAuthor

CALCULATED RISK

KATHERINE RUPLEY

BELLA
BOOKS
2021

Bella Books, Inc.
P.O. Box 10543
Tallahassee, FL 32302

This is a work of fiction. Names, characters, businesses, places, events and incidents are either the products of the author's imagination or used in a fictitious manner. Any resemblance to actual persons, living or dead, or actual events is purely coincidental. The publisher does not have any control over and does not assume any responsibility for author or third-party websites or their content.

Printed in the United States of America on acid-free paper.

First Edition - 2021

Editor: Ann Roberts
Cover Designer: Heather Honeywell
Photo Credit - David Mueller dbmueller photography

ISBN: 978-1-64247-266-0

Acknowledgments

I'd like to thank my mom for starting me on a lifelong love affair with books and who always wanted me to write the great American novel; my wife, Deb, for pushing me to keep going, reading and re-reading my manuscript, and for putting up with all my drama; all my beta readers, Steve Taylor, Ellen Phinney, Suzanne Yanagisawa, Ann Giagni, Jan Schaefer, and Lorna Silva who helped me with all things Spanish; and Barbara Ardinger for the initial edit of my manuscript.

I'd also like to thank Bella Books for taking a chance on a first-time author and putting me in the most excellent hands of Ann Roberts whose gentle and expert coaching taught me so much.

Thanks to the Access Fund (accessfund.org) for supporting, protecting, and encouraging responsible climbing.

Most of all, thanks to all who read. I appreciate you.

Dedication

To Deb, my belay babe!

CHAPTER ONE

Leslie shifted her weight to her left foot before carefully reaching for the small blue handhold above her. Grasping the stiff plastic with two fingers and a thumb, she brought her right foot almost level with her hip and placed it over another small blue wedge bolted to the wall. She rocked her hip over her right foot, gracefully stood and slapped the big metal bar that signified the end of the climb.

"Take," Leslie called, looking down at the woman twenty feet below her on the other end of the rope. There was a rhythm and flow to climbing, a special language of give-and-take between climber and belayer. Leslie respected that precision and stability. Although the risks of a serious fall in a well-lighted, quiet gym were minimal, every climb had its own set of challenges and rewards. She felt the tug on her harness and the rope grew taut. Leaning back from the simulated rock wall into her harness, she allowed herself the feeling of quiet satisfaction. Another puzzle successfully solved.

With quick movements of her wrist and hands, Carrie lowered Leslie to the thick, black rubber mat covering the floor. "You make that look so easy," she said, looking at the climb Leslie had just completed. "Someday," she sighed.

Leslie smiled at her tone and wistful statement. Carrie was a recent addition to Zero G's staff, hired as a junior instructor for kids' birthday parties in the gym. She had the makings of a good climber but needed to learn to trust her body.

Climbs were rated by their difficulty. Leslie had climbed every one of them, mostly on the first attempt, called "flashing" in climbing parlance. She shook her head as she deftly untied the rope from her harness. "You'll get there," she said. "Give yourself some time. You've only been climbing for six months."

"In my mind," Carrie said, "I see me climbing beautifully. It's the body that's caving on me." She unclipped the carabiner and pulled the rope free of the belay device.

"You'll get there," Leslie repeated. "Time for one more belay before I have to leave?" The Los Angeles rock climbing gym was sparsely populated at this time of day. The morning crowd was gone and the lunch group had not yet arrived, so the gym was wide open for exploration.

At Carrie's nod, Leslie ambled over to check out a route one of the new course setters had put up on the opposite wall. Tom, Zero G's manager, had been soliciting new people to set routes and had requested that Leslie evaluate the climbs and the difficulty ratings and give him feedback. Good climbs were hard to set. Each route had strengths and weakness. Technique, balance, strength, reach and stamina all combined in different mixes to provide varying challenges to the climber.

Leslie began tying in.

"Have you met Karen, the new route setter?" Carrie asked.

"No, I don't think so. What does she look like?" Leslie asked, knowing Carrie's habit of trying to set her up on blind dates.

"She's intense. Silky hair, dazzling smile, beautiful deep, dark eyes, lovely muscles…someone even you could appreciate. Best of all, she's family." Carrie had a speculative look in her eyes.

Leslie was looking at the sticker on the wall that gave the climb name, rating, date set, and setter's initials, KN. Checking to make sure Carrie had put on her on belay, she called, "On belay?"

"Belay on," Carrie responded as she tightened up the rope.

"Climbing?"

"Climb on."

Leslie concentrated on the well-marked route, the feel of the simulated rock, the placement of her body and the puzzle to solve. Placing her feet carefully, working her balance, and pulling through smoothly on each hold, she seemed almost to meld with the route. The simulated rock path was deceptive, transitioning from balance moves to a layback which required her to pull with her arms while pushing on the wall with her feet and strength moves to a final dynamic reach at the top. She was breathing heavily by the time she finished. The climb was a good one to end the day with.

"Well," Carrie said, "don't you have anything to say about this wonderful new treasure in our community?"

"No. I haven't seen this new lesbian seventh wonder." Leslie grinned at Carrie's overzealous description as she untied the rope connecting her to the climb. "I'll reserve judgment, although she does set a great climb. What days does she work?"

"No specific days from what I can see," Carrie said. "She just shows up at odd hours, picks a wall and creates. She's done some great things over in the bouldering cave, too."

Carrie enjoyed spreading good news. She was always on the lookout for new blood to expand Zero G's gay and lesbian climbing population.

"Should I tell Pat to put you on a short leash or are you going to behave?" inquired Leslie.

"I wasn't looking for myself, but you on the other hand, you've been single way too long. When was the last time you went out on a date? Any date?"

"I don't have time for dating. You know I barely have time to catch a few hours of climbing for myself between the coaching I do for Tom and my graphic design work. I'm happy. So don't set me up, okay?"

Carrie gave an unenthusiastic nod. "Okay. But for someone so big on climbing, you sure don't take many risks."

"I mean it," said Leslie. "And, for your information, my last date was one you set up for me. You remember Brenda, don't you?"

Carrie threw up her hands. "Okay, okay. You have no sense of humor."

"Well, not for magenta hair and pierced everything. Anyway, I've got to run. Thanks for the climbing. See you Thursday?"

"Thursday," Carrie agreed.

As Carrie left, Tom, the owner of Zero G appeared, waving a sheet of paper. "Alex called from Universal Studios and said he'd be sending a couple of actors over for coaching, a duo known as Jack and Jill. They need to know the moves for a new film that's going into production in February. Right up your alley."

She pulled the paper from his hand. "Jack and Jill? Okay."

"Hey, it's better than kids' birthday parties."

That was true. "I'll call Alex and schedule the times with him."

CJ pelted down the long corridor, leaping over a jagged hole in the floor as a burning ceiling beam swung toward her. Diving to the floor, she rolled and came up running down a maze of hallways. Her long, blond hair streamed out behind her and a cut on her forehead oozed blood. Explosions rocked the walls around her and the force of the air and debris added momentum to her mad dash. Dust and smoke hanging in the air made breathing difficult but she continued her flight to the door at the end of the corridor where a final explosion and hidden wires picked her up and threw her across the room. As she slid to the floor, she willed her body still even as her heart raced and she gasped from the exertion of the run and the force with which she had hit the wall.

"Cut! Good work, CJ," Sam Prescott called. "Okay. That's a wrap for today. People, we'll start shooting scene twelve tomorrow. Everybody be on time."

CJ slowly picked herself up. She knew she was going to have a couple new bruises but she was pleased with the "good work" from Sam. He didn't hand out many compliments but she had hit every mark right on time just as she'd practiced before the explosions and the debris. She had worked on a couple of Sam's films now and knew that although this last scene would be cut up and close-ups of the actor she was portraying would be spliced in, most of the scene would be her. A nice addition to her demo reel.

As she threaded her way through the soundstage and out the backdoor, she called out greetings to a few friends along the way. She slowed when she heard Sally's voice behind her.

"Hey, CJ, that was great! Even knowing that last explosion was going to throw you against that wall, you'd never know it from way you ran the line. But your hair is a fright."

CJ grinned back as she pulled the blond wig off and shook it at Sally. It was hard not to like Sally's boisterous good humor. They had met in college. Working on several films together had cemented their friendship, although no one could understand why. They were as opposite as opposites could be. CJ was action-oriented with shoulder-length dark hair and a self-contained manner. Sally was short and fair and had a need to get in the first, last, and middle word every time. Their choices in partners were equally diverse. Sally liked her men tall, built and quiet, whereas CJ looked for petite, smart and feminine.

"I didn't want to have to wear this horse hair any longer than necessary," CJ said. "I kept thinking it would catch fire and then all the screaming and yelling wouldn't have been faked."

"Go easy with that wig or makeup will have your pay docked."

Sally continued to buzz with local gossip as they wound their way past extra building props to the makeup trailer, where CJ passed in the wig and the prosthetic she had worn for the scene. With some quick words of thanks to Mark and Jim, and an admonition from Jim to be back at five a.m. for the next facial/hair coating for tomorrow's scene, she started off toward her Ford F250. Her mind already on the scene for the next day, she was only peripherally aware of Sally's voice.

"...and Smytheson is looking for a stunt person to work on his latest film."

CJ stopped short; all thoughts of the next day's work forgotten. Jerry Smytheson was the Hollywood director with a capital "D." He had numerous box office smashes to his credit, worked with top actors, and was said to be incredibly loyal to those whose work was good and work habits exceptional. The hype was that he was looking for the Oscar that had eluded him thus far. Getting to work for him would add a necessary boost to her career. Yes, she needed to work for someone like Smytheson. She hated auditioning for work, always soliciting, going to parties just to see who she could meet, who she could get her demo reel in front of. Working for Smytheson, especially if she could impress him, would make her a well-known commodity and would have people coming to her. And it moved her one step closer to her goal of having her own stunt company.

Sally's motor mouth kept moving until she realized she had lost her audience. She stopped and looked at CJ.

"So, what's the new movie and what's he looking for?"

"I was wondering what it would take to wake you up," Sally said. "He's looking for someone to do climbing stunts. He's had a script written to John Grice's book, *On the Edge*. He's got Brendon Lewis and Susan Elliot for the leads."

"Rock climbing," CJ murmured, pushing her hair behind her ears. "Where can I learn about climbing?"

"Scuttlebutt is that Jerry is sending his people over to Zero G, the climbing gym in Santa Monica, for lessons. You might try there."

CJ smiled at her friend. Sally might be a chatterbox but she had great hearing and as the producer's eyes and ears, she heard everything in her work as a producer's assistant.

As they started once more on the trek through the back lot, Sally resumed her monologue, which now centered on a new arrival. "Jennifer is great," she said. "You need to meet her." Sally chattered on, CJ listening with half an ear, as they headed for the trailers. The last thing CJ needed was a romance.

CHAPTER TWO

Reaching the parking lot, Leslie pulled her aging Chevy in beside her boss's beat-up Nissan. One of these days, Sid was going to have to get a new car, or at least a more current used car. The Nissan was held together with duct tape and paper clips. She knew this for a fact. She'd helped him tape his radiator hose just last week. She shook her head, got out of her car and edged past the Nissan, careful not to get rust stains on her slacks.

It wasn't as if he couldn't afford a new automobile. Sid Baker was the head of Mediasoft. He worked outrageous hours to hold the company together but it was a growing concern and had several big-name clients. Each of his seventeen handpicked employees was a jewel in their own right.

Leslie pushed open the door and was immediately confronted by a storm of conversation. Strident voices talking had replaced the normal low-key hum of activity.

"I can't root for the Celtics," George was proclaiming.

"The East Coast? Why the East Coast?" Janet asked in a plaintive voice. "It's cold there. I don't even own a winter coat."

Leslie tapped Ray on the shoulder. "What's going on? What's with George and Janet?"

Ray turned to her. "Sid's sold the business."

Her first irreverent thought was he'd have time to shop for a new car now. "What? He loves this business! How can he sell it?"

"I guess the offer was one he couldn't refuse. He was looking for you earlier. He's hiding in his office."

Leslie wound her way across the half-lit room, dodging the other staff members and computer stations. Sid did not like straight lines so the stations were jumbled around at odd angles. He said it created flexibility of mind. To the unwary, it caused bruises.

When Leslie looked into Sid's office, he had his back to the door, his fingers moving quickly over the keys, email up on the screen.

She rapped her knuckles against the doorframe. "Sorry I'm late," she said. "Traffic was heavier than I expected."

He turned and waved her to a chair. His eyes, behind glasses with small round metal frames, beseeched her to understand his decision.

She gave him a slight smile but no more.

It came out in a rush of words: "I sold the company to AZM."

Although she had heard the news already, it still shocked her. He'd put *everything* into this company. He'd laughed at the way big companies worked and said he'd never sell out. And now? To, of all companies, AZM? AZM was the biggest privately-owned Internet service supplier in the country. It was the one they'd laughed at the most, with its employees in suits and its cookie-cutter approach to programming. She stared at him in disbelief.

"I had to. Leslie, I had no choice. Do you really think I drive that car because I want to?"

She shifted in her chair. Was he a mind reader? How could he have known what she was thinking only moments before? "But I thought everything was going great. We just got two new contracts. One with Warner Brothers—"

"Yeah. But I'm overextended. Those new Sun terminals I bought?" He pointed toward the office area. "And the new software package for web animation? They cost real money."

She nodded.

"I bought them on credit cards."

She was stunned. That was also something he had promised never to do.

"I thought the two new contracts would bring in the necessary capital to bring it all together but there are still the paychecks and rent and utilities, not to mention phone bills. I can't keep it together...Matt's worked the numbers every which way. He told me the credit cards were the wrong approach. But I had to try. It was the last ditch. There's nothing left."

"You love this company," she said softly, noticing how tired he looked. There were dark circles under his eyes and the normally healthy brown of his skin had gray undertones. His broad shoulders slouched forward.

"Yeah." He straightened in his chair. "AZM wants everything and everybody. They just want it all in Boston. The package they're offering is great. Twenty percent increases."

Her eyebrows shot up.

"Yeah." He nodded. "I guess to get the talent, you have to pay the money. Also, they'll give you twenty thousand as a bonus for miscellaneous moving expenses. They'll buy or help you sell your house here or pay to get out of any lease agreement. Help you get a new home and even pack and move you to Boston." He paused. "Plus, they're willing to give everyone two trips out to the East Coast. One to talk to the people they'll be working with, and one five-day trip for house-hunting." He tried to give her a bright smile. "Not a bad offer for everyone."

"Okay," she said, "but where do you fit into the picture?"

"I'll still be a part of things. I'll be heading up the West Coast sales office, but from San Francisco, not Boston." She opened her mouth to say something and he quickly raised a hand to forestall her outburst. "I'll be selling the business but they want the creative staff together. Something about synergy. I tried my best to keep the business here but," he shrugged, "they want everyone but me in Boston." He ran out of steam and stared down at his hands.

After a pause, he looked up. "They need you, Leslie. Bob Craymer specifically asked for you. I think they have a package deal they want to offer you that's different from everyone else's."

She shook her head to clear it. Too much information, too quickly. "I don't know. I'll need some time to think about all that…everything you said. When is all of this happening?"

"Almost immediately. They want to shut down this office in two months' time. They want everyone in Boston ASAP. February is their target. We've stopped with all business until individuals sign with AZM."

"Wow, that's fast. What about the business we've committed to?"

Sid nodded. "I'll be working with AZM on the transition. This business is fast. I sold to AZM, not because they paid me the most, but because of what they offered and how fast they offered it. They want everybody. It's a great deal! Otherwise, we'd all be on the street inside of two weeks. Bob, or his representative, will be calling you later this week. Talk to them."

She nodded and stood. With a final searching look at Sid, she left for her own office. Her energy from the gym workout had drained out while Sid spoke. She had planned her next few years with precision…and now her whole life was up in the air. Working fifty-plus hours a week and climbing the other available hours was a great way of life. In five years the stock options, bonuses, and paychecks would have allowed her an early retirement option, or at least the opportunity to take a long sabbatical to climb all of the mountains and cliffs in the world, which she had researched so lovingly. While she waited and saved, Southern California offered so many climbing options for her precious free time. There were several local crags within an hour's drive. Joshua Tree National Park, one of the world's premier climbing sites, was only three hours away on a Friday night. JT, as it was affectionately called, was a place she loved and enjoyed exploring whenever time permitted.

She sat in her chair, her mind swirling with what she would lose if she left Los Angeles. Beyond the utter chaos of moving and leaving all her normal daily patterns, her family was here. Mom and Dad lived a few hours away in Solvang. Close enough for a visit but far enough away that they couldn't just drop in unexpectedly, or they hadn't so far. Travel costs from Boston clinked against her mental savings bucket.

Her mind came back again to climbing, her one major passion. All her climbing buddies were here. She shook herself out of the endless circle of unhelpful thoughts.

What was in Boston? She couldn't think of anything beyond the Boston Celtics and Bunker Hill. What about the surrounding area? New York was close by, wasn't it? The Gunks was another internationally known climbing area located somewhere in New York, a place she had heard of but never visited.

She turned to her computer. She knew the Gunks' real name started with an S, but after trying several different spellings she gave up and just typed "Gunks" in the search tab. Several sites popped up immediately. Ah, there it was—New York State's Shawangunks, located in New Paltz. Now she had a city. She quickly opened another browser window and entered Boston, MA, and New Paltz, NY. The search engines showed her several websites with distance and directions. The centers of the two cities were 216.1 miles apart, with an approximate travel time of three hours and forty-three minutes. She checked out the map. The route ran right through the heart of Hartford, Connecticut. Well, that couldn't be good on a Friday night. She looked more carefully at the map and spotted the train tracks. Maybe she could take a train. After all, wasn't that the way you got around on the East Coast?

Going back to the previous website, she clicked on a site for an adventure climbing group specializing in Gunks climbing. She roamed around the site, looking at pictures and reading local information. Finally, seeing an email address for additional information, she sent a query asking for travel options from Boston to the Gunks. After sending the message, she sat back, content that she'd done something proactive.

She knew no productive work was going to happen today, so she pulled out the slip of paper Tom had given her and studied the phone number. Even if she did decide to go to Boston, she could take the coaching job. She needed something to get her mind away from more endless circles of thinking about her future. This could do the trick.

CHAPTER THREE

Two days later, CJ found herself searching for a parking place. The small parking lot had limited gym parking and parking on the densely populated street was next to impossible. She quickly edged her black Ford F250 pickup into a slot just recently occupied by a delivery truck.

On one side were two-story apartment complexes, while the other side was made up of small postproduction offices on two floors and a few warehouses. The gym was located at the end of the offices in a three-story warehouse. Since there was no sidewalk in front of the warehouse, she made her way down the middle of the parking lot.

When she pushed open the door of Zero G, her senses were immediately assaulted by the smells of sweat, chalk, and blasts of eighties' rock music against the hum of conversations. She also noted the openness of the room, which was well lit by overhead LED fluorescent bulbs. She headed for the front desk where a lanky teenager took money from a pair of women who were asking about gym memberships.

As she waited for his attention, she focused on the gym itself, taking in the great expanses of colorful fake rocks with strangely shaped pieces fastened to the walls with large hex-head bolts, making abstract patterns on the manmade outcroppings. Ropes hung down from large black bars like individual strands of drying homemade pasta. Several ropes had one end tied in some kind of knot. The other ends of these ropes lay in an untidy heap on the thick rubber mats. She could make out a few large pieces of what looked like white duct tape on the wall with words like Jerome's Revenge, Green Hornet, and Stairway to Heaven written on them.

"Can I help you?" said a male voice, deeper than that of the youth who was working the desk.

CJ swiveled to face a man of indeterminate age, anywhere between an old forty and a young sixty. He was a few inches under six feet and had well-muscled arms, shaggy blond hair, and a welcoming smile.

"Yes," she said. "I need to learn to how to climb. Quickly."

The man studied her for a moment as if waiting for more information. When she said nothing else, he said, "We have a beginner's class starting in an hour. Do you have your own equipment?"

"No, what will I need?"

He led her back to the desk. "You'll need a harness." He pulled one from a pegboard on the wall. "What's your shoe size?"

"Eight."

He grabbed a pair of shoes from under the counter. "You can wear them with socks or not. Your choice. Socks take away your feel, but it's a personal preference. Try them on. The shoes should be very snug but not uncomfortable. You'll be wearing them for about three hours."

CJ took the shoes. They looked like contorted ballet slippers. The toes were covered with a stiff, black, rubbery material, as were the bottoms and the heels. As there were no chairs in sight, she took the shoes over toward a free wall and sat on the floor where she pulled off her own shoes and socks and put on the climbing shoes. They were extremely tight and seemed to mold to her feet, but she knew she could endure them for three hours. She needed to learn climbing quickly and if it helped the process, she could be uncomfortable.

She collected her shoes and socks and stood. Returning to the counter she said, "These shoes will do fine. Do I need anything else?"

"That's the basics and come with the class fee. A chalk bag can be helpful if your hands sweat."

She didn't think she had sweaty hands but she wasn't willing to forego any aid or technique that would help her learn what she needed to know. She knew enough to trust the experts. After the chalk bag with a one-inch black strap with a quick release fastener for strapping around her waist was added to the pile, she paid the fees.

"Feel free to explore the gym and try out some bouldering until class starts," the man said. Noting her blank look, he added, "Bouldering is climbing done at a height that if you fall off, you don't tend to get seriously hurt. It's also done off rope. The line of holds you see going around the gym at about eye level in that lime green are considered a bouldering traverse. You can also try the bouldering cave located in the back of the gym. Check out the shoes and check out the rock. Class starts at seven, which gives you about ten minutes to play." He smiled again. "My name's Tom. If you need anything, let me know, or one of these temporarily working climbers can help you out." He pointed at the teenager, now returning from the back room with a dozen pairs of shoes tucked under his arms.

CJ thanked him and wandered into the gym area. Along the wall near the locker rooms were cubbyholes for street gear. She deposited her shoes and socks, then turned to watch the activity in the gym. The area was full of people calling greetings to one another, shouting encouragement and giving grunts of exertion. It seemed very festive, kind of like a local pub without the alcohol and the food, although there were a few PowerBar wrappers in evidence.

Several climbers in the bouldering area looked like strange spider people as they positioned themselves on the walls and crept slowly upward, moving only one of four limbs at a time, their bodies twisting and turning slowly in an internal rhythm. A hot pink, skintight bodysuit caught her attention as she noticed a very long, loose-limbed, ebony man with incredibly sleek muscles edging into view from the other side of the rock. His fluid, seemingly effortless motion pulled him around the rock and up under an overhanging ledge. His hips were tight against the wall, his body aligned for the small holds and manmade cracks of the ledge. As several people stopped to watch, he pulled through to the top. A splattering of applause broke out. He swung outward, and with the lightness of a cat, righted himself, hit the ground with a gymnast's ease, and bowed to his audience.

"Joe," said a voice nearby, "stop showing off and get ready for your class."

CJ turned to find Tom standing behind her. He angled a thumb and smiled at the now grinning Joe. "He's your instructor for tonight. He's also a drama queen so enjoy the show and learn what you can."

When CJ put out her hand to shake Joe's, he turned it over and kissed the back in a courtly gesture from another era, as if that were the standard greeting for climbers. She was slightly taken aback but took it in stride. She was used to the eccentricities of actors. How much weirder could climbers be?

Joe and Tom both laughed at her expression.

"Let's go meet the rest of tonight's victims," Joe said, dropping her hand with a wink and nodding at three other people near the front wall who were trying to put on their rented climbing harnesses. They were having problems sorting through the leg loops and waist straps.

He spent the next ten minutes getting everyone into their harnesses and climbing shoes and explaining some of the gym's safety rules. After the potential climbers were geared up and settled into comfortable sprawls on the floor, Joe formally started the class.

"Climbing is more a mind game than a physical one," he began. "It teaches confidence, harmony, freedom, flexibility. Climbing is like a physical puzzle. You put the moves together in your head and then your body plays them through to the conclusion. Sometimes it's not pretty, but sometimes it's elegant." He paused.

"Okay, let's get started. First, the knots. The most important knot you'll ever tie in climbing is the figure-eight knot. Why, you ask? Because it's the knot that will stop the rope from coming off you and dropping you to the ground." He flipped his wrist and formed the eight with his hands. "After you create your eight, take the rope end through your harness, then follow the rope end back through the knot until you have two eights on top of each other. And then as a finishing touch, tie a double knot to make sure the figure-eight stays in place. You can tell if you've got it right." He held up the rope and showed his class the two figure-eights lying next to each other.

After a couple of misses, CJ figured out the tying technique. While the others were still working out the knot, she repeated the exercise several times. She also made a mental note to get some rope and practice at home until she had it down. Not being able to tie this knot easily would be a dead giveaway that she wasn't a climber.

Next, Joe went on to explain the verbal exchanges between climber and belayer. CJ memorized them quickly. Belaying was the next exercise. The group used a simple Air Traffic Controller, commonly called an ATC, which was a machined piece of metal with two uniform holes for the rope and a loop to lock onto a harness via a locking carabiner that allowed a belayer to quickly stop a climber from falling. The belayer used friction in the device by simply and firmly moving the end of the rope not attached to the climber below his waist and holding tight. The group then had fun climbing up several feet and jumping off, trying to catch their belay partners sleeping. CJ had heard about how corporations sent teams that were having difficulties with communication and trust for a day of climbing. Belaying was a full-on trust event. You had to trust that the person on the other end of the rope was paying attention and had the skills to help you. It was the same with stunt work: inattention could get you seriously crippled, or worse, dead.

"Did any of you notice the interesting names on the climbs?" Joe asked. Several people nodded. "Each climb has a name and a rating. Coming up with a cool name is part of the fun of designing or finding a route, matching a name to a climb." He pointed at a nearby climb named "Green Hornet 5.4." The climb was made up of lots of big green holds. "This is one of the easiest climbs in the gym. The 5.4 is based on an outdoor climbing scale. The five rating is for any climbs that need ropes for safety because a fall could seriously injure or even kill you." He made a sweeping gesture around the room. "This gym has climbs rated from 5.4, which are fairly easy, to 5.11b. Spiderman time."

As expected, the class laughed.

"Climbing in a gym is controlled. Falling even from a 5.11b in here won't kill you, but you could get seriously hurt if you fall wrong. Outdoor climbing is in a whole different class. Mistakes outdoors could get you or your belayer seriously injured and even killed. Take a class, learn the skills, be safe." He looked at each of them in turn, and then with a wide smile said, "Enough gloom and doom. Let's climb!" He pointed to two climbs, both rated 5.4, with big, bright, neon holds. "Tie in and climb on."

The next forty-five minutes were spent on the wall. While she was on the wall climbing and belaying, CJ kept questioning Joe on technique. *Bend your knees, keep your arms as straight as possible, lift your weight with your legs, flow from move to move, work the angles, pivot, balance, find your center, hips to the wall, trust your feet.*

By the end of the forty-five minutes, she had figured out a couple of things but she knew that she'd have to work hard to make it look easy.

"Joe, who can I get to help me progress really fast?"

"Well, yours truly, of course," he preened. "But hold that thought, I'm too busy. The best climber here is Leslie McAllister. She gives lessons but she's hard. Don't work with her if you don't have a full commitment, 'cause, girl, she'll chew you up and there won't be nothing left. Climbing isn't a pastime with her. It's a religion."

CJ nodded. She understood Leslie's philosophy. Commitment she had in spades. "Thanks, Joe. I've learned a lot. See you around the gym."

Walking back to the front desk, she waved at Tom. "How do I get set up to have private lessons with Leslie?"

Tom looked at her for a moment. "You must have impressed Joe if he gave you her name. Are you sure you want to make that commitment?"

CJ nodded. "I'm sure."

He took her rented equipment, rummaged through the desk, found a piece of paper and wrote a number on it. "Call her up. She'll decide whether or not she wants to take you on."

CJ was surprised by Tom's comment but she took the paper. "I'll call her. Thanks for your help, Tom."

On the way home, she stopped at the local bookstore and picked up a couple of books on climbing. Then she drove home to figure out how she could wow Brad Carter, who was in her mind the best stunt coordinator in the business and the man she most wanted to emulate and possibly work with someday.

CHAPTER FOUR

Leslie, her mind on her Boston offer, absently lined up her Lego *Star Wars* figurines on her desk. Sid had been correct when he'd said AZM really wanted her. Her package included a fifty-percent raise, stock options, and a fifty-thousand signing bonus. The raise sounded great and it was a hefty raise from industry standard. Her previous salary had been low as it was a startup with potential based on the company going public sometime in the future. The fifty-thousand meant she could pay off her remaining student debt, buy a new car, or set aside some money for a down payment on a condo and the path to the stability she craved. Boston, she thought, was cold and far from her life in Los Angeles.

As she pushed Chewbacca to the end of the lineup and reached for a pad of paper, her cell phone buzzed and she checked the phone number. It wasn't one she recognized. She was tempted to let it go to voice mail, but had been told to expect a phone call from the two stunt people from *On the Edge*. Hitting accept, she said, "Leslie."

"Hi, Leslie, this is CJ Broadmore. Joe gave me your name and said you could get me climbing like an expert—fast. When can we get started?"

Leslie's mind tried to process what she had just heard. Joe? She thought Tom or Alex made the connection, not Joe.

"Hello? Did I lose you?"

"No, I'm here. What is it you want to get out of my coaching?"

There was a pause, and then CJ said, "I want to understand climbing and the fluid motions that make climbing the poetry of strength and elegance."

Well, that sure sounded canned. "Really?"

CJ laughed. "I want to climb with enough competency to impress Jerry Smytheson."

Even Leslie knew who Jerry was. She suspected everyone in the film industry or anyone who watched movies knew who he was. But did she have the time for this? Alex had lined up two people he'd called Jack and Jill for her to work with—though she understood those weren't their real names—she didn't question the strangeness of Hollywood. Did she want to take on another newbie climber with aspirations of grandeur?

"Do you know the basics?"

"I took Joe's beginner class yesterday. I've been reading up."

"And Joe recommended you call me?"

"Yes."

Leslie sighed. "Okay. Meet me at Zero G at ten Sunday morning. Let's see what you've got. No promises. My schedule is tight and Tom has already made commitments for me." *And I'm probably going to be leaving town.*

As she put down the phone, she picked up her pen and began her list… More money, job security, stability, new car, no debt… all the things she wanted. Maybe Boston would be a good move for her.

CHAPTER FIVE

CJ stared at the phone in her hand and thought about what she had said. Both reasons were correct. She did see the poetry of motion in climbing. She had watched enough YouTube videos to see how physically and mentally challenging climbing could be. And there were so many types of climbing. Bouldering—without rope—limited to about twenty feet or less of falling... ouch! Top-rope climbing, where an anchor was set at the top of the climb that allowed a climber to climb to the top with a belayer ensuring their safety. Traditional climbing, where protective gear was placed in crevices along the climb by the lead climber and the rope clipped into a carabiner attached to the protective gear as the lead climber progressed upward. Both traditional and top rope climbing had a belayer minding the rope and monitoring the climber's progress. The final type of climbing was free soloing. She had checked out The National Geographic award-winning film, *Free Solo*, of Alex Honnold's free solo of Yosemite's El Capitan which had been equal parts awe-inspiring and terrifying. Long climbs with no placed protection and no ropes. It all looked dangerous for the skilled and downright hazardous for the unskilled. She didn't need to know everything, only how to look like she did. She needed to impress Jerry Smytheson.

Jerry, she knew, could spot a phony a mile away. He was a perfectionist and she didn't want her efforts, if she did get a chance to audition, to end up on the cutting room floor. It was a sad fact that action movies made the big money, but only if she could break into the big leagues. She had done some big movies but only her hands or a few minor elements had appeared in the final cut. She needed more screen time to really make it.

Stunt people had a limited shelf life thanks to the wear and tear on their bodies, but a good stunt person could increase their longevity if they had the name recognition and the creativity to pull a team together to coordinate and structure the stunts the director wanted. She knew that she had that skill set, if only she could make the name. She needed Leslie to help her make that leap.

She also needed to ping Sally for more information. Sally would know how to get the script and figure out who the stunt director would be. If a stunt coordinator had already been selected, CJ would need to replace one of the currently planned stunt people. That posed a challenge. Stunt coordinators liked their own people. She'd need to find out who they were and how attached to the project they were.

Keys rattling in the door halted her mental checklist. Joannie entered, bags on each arm, her phone under her chin.

"Can you believe Jake and Bill's fight last night? I thought Bill would tear Jake's head off his shoulders." She waved a bag at CJ and headed for the kitchen.

Joannie was a professional personal chef. She made custom meals and meal plans for the celebrity and film industry elite. She had also been CJ's one-time squeeze but they had found they were better as friends than lovers.

As CJ heard kitchen cabinets opening and closing, she knew she'd be on the receiving end of another culinary experiment. Luckily for her, most were wonderful, with only a few "flops" in the mix.

She headed for the fridge and a beer. "So how are the twins today? Still trying to confuse you?"

Joannie turned on the gas burner and slid the onions and garlic into the skillet. "The twins are easy to figure out. They just don't know they're easy to figure out," she grinned, "so I play along and everyone is happy. I think you'll be interested to hear the other, more interesting news." She paused for effect, continuing to add ingredients.

Knowing that Joannie liked to create drama, CJ seldom encouraged her, but she also knew Joannie was privy to really good intelligence. "Okay, I'll bite."

"You're going to owe me big-time for this one."

"Dinner at California Pizza Kitchen or Mélisse," naming one of the premiere restaurants in Santa Monica.

Joannie's eyebrows shot up. "Mélisse, and it's worth it. Brad Carter is the stunt coordinator for *On the Edge*."

CJ clapped her hands together, then swept Joannie up into a big hug.

"Hey—I'm cooking here," Joannie squeaked.

CJ ignored her. "That's fantastic! He's awesome. And he knows my work. Now I know who my competition is and I've got a chance. Jack and Jill." Jack and Jill weren't their real names. The pair had gotten those names after rolling down a particularly horrible hill when doubling for Brad Pitt and Angelina Jolie in a sequel to *Mr. and Mrs. Smith* that nobody had ever seen. The shoot had been canceled for lack of a plot and nothing remained except for that one stunt.

Regardless, Jack and Jill were highly rated in the business and came as a matched set. She didn't think they knew rock climbing but she'd need to beat them to the punch and get Brad to recognize her skills. If nothing else, as a key backup.

Yes, she needed to focus on climbing. She left the kitchen and headed back to her stack of climbing magazines and YouTube videos.

CHAPTER SIX

CJ was at Zero G early. Directors expected punctuality and the no-nonsense attitude she had heard on the phone call made her think that Leslie would appreciate it as well. There were a few other climbers lounging around making small talk which stopped when a tall, lanky woman with short brown finger-combed hair, in baggy climbing pants and a hoodie appeared from around the corner of the building. Her easy stride was athletic and confident.

She greeted a few of the regulars before turning to size up CJ. Her look was friendly but there was a look of appraisal as well.

"CJ?" Leslie held out her hand.

CJ nodded, smiled, and shook Leslie's outstretched hand.

"I appreciate you getting here on time," Leslie said as she unlocked the door for CJ and the regulars. "Let me get set up and I'll join you in the bouldering area. Do you have shoes? A harness?"

"Got gear at REI yesterday," CJ said, swinging her backpack off her shoulders.

Leslie nodded at one of the regulars, a young man with dreads and a carefully manicured beard. He walked to the light panel and turned on the lights in the various sections of the gym.

"Go ahead and put on your shoes," she told CJ. "The harness can wait." She walked behind the counter and waved at the other regulars. "Do some warm-up stretches," she added. "I need to set up the desk."

CJ headed over to the bouldering cave, where she stashed her backpack in a nearby gear cubby. CJ surveyed the multicolored plastic grips affixed to the overhanging wall at various heights. It looked very much like a mental puzzle, if you followed the path through any specific color. As she sat on the floor to begin her stretches, she watched Leslie out of the corner of her eye wanting to get a sense of the woman who potentially held her future in her hands. She was doing something behind the counter and talking animatedly to a young Asian man who had joined her at the register. She had good bone structure with even features and expressive eyebrows which showed her emotions. Years of having dealt with all kinds of movie people had given CJ a fairly good feel for judging people quickly and correctly. Leslie had star quality. She just didn't do anything to promote it. Interesting.

Several minutes later, now wearing her rock-climbing shoes, Leslie appeared before CJ. "So," she said, "what is it you expect from me?"

CJ looked up into Leslie's golden-brown eyes, started to reply, and then became suddenly tongue-tied as she noticed the slight green flecks in the brown. When Leslie blinked, CJ was released from her reverie. *What was the question?* She had come prepared with an answer but it didn't seem appropriate now. Leslie's eyes demanded honesty. "I'm a stunt person. I want to work on *On the Edge*, which starts shooting soon, and I need you to make me look great."

Leslie's eyes appraised CJ. They seemed to reach into her soul. She blinked again, then laughed. "How much time do I have? Great by today or do I have until tomorrow?"

CJ laughed with her. "How about by the end of the week? I'm all yours until then."

"All mine?"

CJ's heart skipped a beat. "Yes." And she returned Leslie's smile with one of her own.

What's going on? CJ asked herself. She never flirted, especially with a woman she didn't know. She didn't even know if this woman was gay or single. But she didn't seem to be able to stop herself. This wasn't going the way she'd thought it would.

"We'd better get started. Today the gym. Tomorrow real rock. You'll never be great until you can understand the way granite, or rather monzogranite, feels under your hands and feet. You're not ready for that yet but you haven't given me much time. And looking good is more important than being good. Or at least that's true for film, not real life."

Leslie was still speaking and CJ tried to focus. "Try the traverse and let's see your form," she said. "It's the path around the wall. Parallel to the floor. You don't go up, just across."

CJ stepped up to the wall and grabbed the smallest handholds, then stepped up on the footholds and promptly popped off the wall. Stumbling slightly, she shot an embarrassed glance back at Leslie and tried again, this time picking a larger hold with a better grip. She proceeded to move along the wall using the three-point rule that Joe had taught her: keep three points of contact on the wall at all times. And move slowly and methodically.

Just as CJ's arms were starting to give out, Leslie called, "Stop." CJ was so intent on what she was doing that she had completely forgotten Leslie. She twisted to look at her and almost lost her footing. When Leslie's hand came up to steady her, she could feel the heat of her hand through her tank top.

"See how you're holding on to the wall?" Leslie asked. "Where are you taking your weight? In your arms or in your shoulders and back? Can you hold your current position?"

CJ felt the strain in her biceps. She was going to come off the wall for real if she didn't move soon.

Again, Leslie's hand was on her back. "Relax your arms. Bend your knees a little, hips into the wall. And breathe."

CJ could immediately feel the pressure in her arms easing. She sighed in relief. It felt awkward. She reoriented her feet on the footholds and pulled her hips closer to the wall. Some of the awkwardness left her stance.

"Good," Leslie commented. "Remember that. Come off the wall now. Did you get certified to belay?"

CJ nodded, pointing at the plastic card attached to her harness. "Joe was very thorough."

"On both the grigri and the ATC?"

"Yep, Joe said something about ATC were for real climbers and grigris were for the gym. He taught me both since I told him about my need to come off as an expert climber."

Leslie snorted at this. "Real climbers do use grigris but I like the feel and control an ATC gives you." She walked to another section of the wall that was filled with colorful holds and picked up a rope that went through an anchor high up on a roof beam. As she began tying in, she said, "Set up to belay me. I need you to pay attention to the belay, as my safety is in your hands, but also watch what I do and how I move, especially watch my body and the positions of my hips and hands."

CJ's eyes flicked over Leslie's hips and the curve of her butt in the harness. She felt her heart beat a little faster, though she wasn't sure if it was from her awareness of Leslie's superb body or the thought that she had this woman's life literally in her hands. *Girl, get your head in the game and out of the gutter.*

Leslie finished tying in and then had CJ check the figure-eight, the finishing knot and then her harness. Leslie checked CJ's harness, anchor and her ATC configuration to make sure she was ready. Then Leslie turned to the wall and studied the various routes denoted by the differently-colored pieces of tape next to the simulated rocks. She selected her route and turned to CJ. "On belay?" she asked.

"Belay on."

"Climbing?"

"Climb on."

Leslie stepped onto the wall. Although the holds looked small and awkward, she seemed almost to flow up the wall. She moved slowly, deliberately, her hips snug against the wall, her feet and hands precisely placed each time. There was no wasted motion.

It looks so easy, CJ thought, but deceptively so. She could see that the holds were not placed for ease but for position, so movement was always up, just not directly up. There seemed to be expanses of emptiness followed by multiple pieces to choose from and confuse the climber. When Leslie's hand and feet came together on just such a placement, she looked up, sighted, and leaped like a leopard to a hold four feet up. She caught it with one hand as her feet smacked on the open wall. She quickly but gracefully put her other hand on a nearby grip and tagged the top beam, signaling the end of the climb.

"Take," she called to CJ.

Startled, CJ quickly pulled in the excess rope that she had failed to mind in the sheer wonder of what she had witnessed in the last ten feet of Leslie's climb. Leslie looked down and seemed to note her actions, waiting for the belay to be tight again and release her hold, lying back in her harness to be slowly belayed down.

"I can't do that," CJ stated after Leslie's feet were once more on the floor.

"Maybe not today, but if you listen and learn, that could be you in a couple of," she paused for effect, "years." She laughed at CJ's crestfallen look. "Let's see how good we can get you in the next few days."

Leslie compared CJ's efforts with the other stunt team. She had gotten a phone call from a man right after CJ's phone call, but she hadn't liked his attitude. She had met with the team the previous night. The man who had introduced himself as Jack, though she knew it wasn't his real name, had questioned her every statement, not with the purpose of learning, but as if to push her buttons and challenge her capabilities. She didn't know what was up with that, but she did know she didn't have to put up with it. After letting Jack try a fairly simple climb and watching him muscle his way up multiple times without using any of the techniques she had explained to him, she decided he looked like a fireman climbing a ladder but with less grace. She hadn't expected Jack to be good at doing everything she'd told him, but there was no grace in the way he used brute-force to make his way to the top. She had then let his partner, Jill, belay her and had provided a running commentary on the techniques and instruction she had given them both as she easily completed the climb. Jill seemed to get it and seemed fairly competent, but Leslie had already had enough, so she palmed them off on Joe. Maybe Jack would learn better from a man. She felt sorry for Jill but the pair came as a matched set.

Now, after switching roles, Leslie watched CJ step up to the new, easier climb she had indicated. She stepped CJ through the motions and the strategies of the climb. "Given the time we have, the purpose is to make it look hard. And easy. The climb—hard and scary. Your moves through it—easy and smooth." Leslie paused. "I can't make you a 5.11 climber in a week but maybe we can make you a competent 5.8-5.10a climber in a gym and maybe a 5.8 climber outside. From what you've said about the movie, some of the climbing will be on rope and some will be free solo climbing. Based on the climbs, they'll probably always have you roped in for safety's sake and remove the rope later, using Hollywood magic. The climbing techniques are similar but slightly different. Risks that you might take on rope, you most likely would not take as a free climber. I'll teach you some of the jump techniques in case that's what they want. The moves are showy and look hard."

Leslie had CJ do the same climb again until she could see CJ's strength beginning to flag. But CJ was getting better and listening to her instructions. This might work.

"Let's call it a day," Leslie finally said. "You've been at it for three hours. You must be starved. I know I am and I put out a lot less effort."

At that moment CJ's stomach gurgled. They both laughed.

"Looks like the boss has spoken. Can I take you to lunch so we can discuss your plan for making me look like an inspired climber? I managed to get a meeting with Brad Carter, the *On the Edge* stunt coordinator, for Monday. That means I have until then to learn what I need to wow him, or at least wow him enough to back up Jack and Jill."

Leslie could feel her lips twitch in reaction to CJ's statement.

"What?" CJ said. "Don't tell me you've met them?"

Leslie merely replied, "Where are you taking me for lunch? Anything but Italian. I love it, but I always totally overeat."

CHAPTER SEVEN

"You need experience on real rock," Leslie said as she bit into her grilled shrimp taco. CJ's choice had been a first-rate, hole-in-the-wall Mexican restaurant near Zero G. "I suggest that we go to Joshua Tree and immerse ourselves in all things climbing. I can teach you way more there than in a gym. Plus, I can teach you anchoring, which will be important as you set up the stunts for the filming. Safety is paramount. Even a fall from a very short distance can cause serious injury."

CJ checked her mental calendar. "I can do that," she said, making a note of the people and appointments she'd need to move.

"There are a number of hotels in Yucca Valley that are near the entrance to Joshua Tree, or JT, as it's known to the climbing community. I hear there's a famous theme motel there, too," said Leslie, wiggling her eyebrows.

"Sounds interesting."

"It's about a three-hour drive from LA to the Yucca Valley and another hour to where I'll be camping in the park. It's manageable but time consuming. If you stay in a motel, you'll lose a lot of the feel of JT. Tom has a small RV that he lets me use. It's from the eighties but it still runs great, even if it gets terrible mileage. You can stay with me if you'd like. We won't be spending much time in the RV. Our focus will be on climbing."

CJ had never been much of a camper and she didn't know if she could be in such close proximity to Leslie without jumping her bones. Other than the casual wordplay, she wasn't even sure Leslie was a lesbian, although she did give off the vibe. One mistake back in college had forever prevented CJ from guessing about sexuality.

"Why don't I try a hotel in Yucca Valley," she said, "and see how that works? I can always join you later," CJ paused, "if it proves too complicated."

Leslie nodded slowly.

The silence following CJ's suggestion had gone on too long. "Is there a problem?" she asked. She felt that Leslie had wanted a different answer.

"Nope," Leslie said. "I'll be trying for a campsite at Hidden Valley. It's a little bit of a climbing mecca. We won't have to go far to climb unless we want to. I like to start early, though, so make sure you take travel time into account if you're coming from town. Also make sure you have water. The last available water is at the park entrance. There's none in the park and it's dry there, so you'll be drinking more than you expect."

CJ nodded. "Got it. Bring water and don't be late."

Leslie nodded. "Campsites are first come, first serve, but going on a Tuesday, I should be able to score a campsite at Hidden Valley. JT is high desert. It's November, which means it can be cold in the mornings and evenings. Bring a jacket or fleece or both. If you change your mind about staying in town, the RV has two sleep areas...if you were worried about me jumping your bones."

CJ could feel heat in her cheeks but regrouped and smiled at Leslie. "I'll keep that in mind."

CHAPTER EIGHT

On the appointed Tuesday, Leslie arrived early at the entrance to Joshua Tree National Park. She loved the park at this time of day when the color on the rocks was rich and warm. As she drove down Park Boulevard toward the turnoff for the campgrounds, she marveled at the Joshua trees, which gave the park its name, scattered across the landscape. On the left side of the road, the rock formations looked like the gods had been playing and left huge boulders piled one on top of another.

It was such a magical park. It had even been honored with the Dark Sky Park status by the International Dark-Sky Association. At night with no city lights to interfere, the sky was a clear midnight blue with the Milky Way prominent across a sky filled with stars. Leslie wasn't very good at meditation, but she could sit on a boulder in the evening for long stretches of time just enjoying the beauty. It was a peaceful, calm place. Just what she needed.

The Hidden Valley campground was fuller than she's anticipated, but she found a campsite near the trail to The Blob, a rock formation so named by a climber in the fifties or sixties. The RV was not the one she had planned on bringing to the park. Tom had upgraded since she had last borrowed his rig and the upgrade was great. His 2016 Thor Chateau 22E was easy to drive, provided a few welcome luxuries, had better gas mileage and was still small enough to fit Hidden Valley's length restrictions. She could have just put up a tent but she really liked having access to a shower, a toilet for the middle of the night (no trekking to the public restrooms for her at two a.m.), and not worrying about food storage.

Setup was easy and quickly completed. She walked to the camp registration station, paid her camping fee and texted CJ her campsite number. Now it was time to climb. Even though she wanted to stay close so that when CJ came she'd be easy to find, it was hard not to wander off to Turtle Rock which was farther off the trail. She had brought a foldable crash pad, which looked like a thin mini-futon, for bouldering. She pulled it out of the back of the RV and shrugged it on like an unwieldy backpack, pulling the straps tight. Then she headed out to explore the area and see who else might be climbing this week.

It was around eleven a.m., when she was playing on the Stem Gem Boulder, that she got the text that CJ had arrived in camp. She completed the mantel, a sideways motion across the rock face that brought her to the crux move at the top of the boulder problem she had been working on, then jumped down and landed on the crash pad. Collecting her gear, she headed back to the RV, where she found CJ sitting in one of the lawn chairs she had put up outside the camper. Her feet were propped casually on a nearby rock.

"Beautiful morning. So calm and peaceful here," CJ said as she walked into camp.

Leslie sat in the second lawn chair and nodded. "Joshua Tree has that effect on people."

"It's a little chillier than I expected. I've always heard the desert's hot and dry."

"It can be. JT is high desert, and this time of year we get a little reprieve. Late November through January, it can be downright cold. I like the RV and all the blankets I can pile on. Did you get the intel from Brad on what kind of climbing will be in the film?"

"Yep." CJ leaned her head back and ran her fingers through her hair. "Long crack climbs, pinnacles and the leaps you mentioned."

"Hmmmm. And all I need to do is make you look good, not just competent?" Leslie was gazing at the line of CJ's neck.

CJ looked up and caught Leslie's eyes. "I'd like to be both."

She smiled and stood. "Well, then, let's get started. You're not going to be either just sitting in that chair unless you're going for a different kind of stunt." She pulled a second crash pad out of the back of the camper, then grabbed a small duffel bag. She handed the crash pad to CJ. "Here. Put this on and let's go do some bouldering. I need to teach you proper hand techniques and footwork. You can spot a bad climber by their footwork."

CJ pulled the crash pad onto her shoulders and followed her out of the campsite.

"Do you know where the filming is going to take place?"

"Per Brad, right here in JT. He said there were a couple of multi-pitch climbs that he thought would work for the desired shots."

"JT has everything but I would've thought they'd want to go more exotic."

"I think the original movie was going to be done in Thailand but the director is taking the picture more dramatic—acting dramatic versus cinematic dramatic—because he wants to stay closer to home. A 'local makes good' kind of story."

"There is some good climbing in Bishop and Yosemite in California."

Leslie slowed her pace as she realized that CJ was having trouble keeping up.

"Those locations were mentioned. They may come back up but JT is the current favorite."

"I'm glad Jerry wants to stay local. I think he'll be surprised at how much visual impact Joshua Tree will give the film. And you lucked out because I know Joe won't be bringing your friends out here. He's got an aversion to outdoor climbing. He almost grabbed a rattlesnake once."

CJ stumbled. "Rattlesnakes?"

"Relax, it's November. Brisk weather. There won't be any rattlesnakes moving around at this time of year."

CJ was walking beside her now and staring into the rocks and crevices around them as if she expected to see a rattler waiting just for her.

Leslie laughed. "Joe doesn't believe it either. He expects them to be waiting just for him. Thus, we won't see Jack or Jill or Joe. J3. Now that's catchy." She surveyed the surrounding area. There were other climbers in this part of the park but they were scattered and there was plenty of open space to set up and climb. She knew The Old Woman rock formation had some interesting bouldering problems, so she headed for School Boulder near the bottom of the east face of The Old Woman. No one there, which was good, as it was a popular area because of its proximity to the campgrounds.

CJ watched as Leslie shrugged off her crash pad and laid it precisely near a boulder patchworked with white chalk marks. After studying the boulder for a long minute, she gestured for CJ to give her the one she carried and she placed it to support the first one.

"Protection from a fall or a bad step. We'll move them as needed for whatever problem we're working." Her attention was once more fixed on the rock in front of her.

CJ watched what Leslie was doing and noticed the flex and flow of her muscles through the thin hoodie she wore. Her legs were encased in an old, worn pair of Prana pants that looked well loved. Sexy, CJ thought. Just the right blend of strength, confidence, and easy appeal. *Mind on climbing, not your under-sexed body. It's been a long time between girlfriends.*

When Leslie turned to CJ's watchful eyes, she cocked her head to the side and grinned like a kid who'd been caught out past dark. "Sorry, I love to work through problems in my head before I climb onto the rock," she said as she handed her a chalk bag out of the duffel bag. "You'd be surprised how sweaty your hands get climbing. Might be the fear factor. Also gives you something to do between moves and while you try to get some strength back in your hands and biceps."

CJ accepted the chalk bag and clipped it around her waist. She also unclipped her climbing shoes from her harness. She probably wouldn't be needing her harness today but she felt that she needed to get comfortable wearing it and making it part of herself. She sat on a boulder, pulled off her Salomon trail shoes and put on the tight-fitting Sportiva climbing shoes she had just purchased.

Nodding her approval, Leslie tossed CJ a helmet she had pulled out of her duffel. "Did you check out the YouTube videos I sent you last night?"

"Yep. I especially liked the ones where you sit on the ground to start." CJ pulled on the helmet and cinched the strap.

"Not far to fall if you come off on the first move." Leslie chuckled and pulled on her own helmet. "Seriously, the boys can muscle their way through a lot of their failings. We can't, at least not if we want to climb for very long. We have our strength in our legs. And our flexibility."

CJ understood where Leslie was headed. She had spent a lot of time with stuntmen and knew how much they relied on sheer strength to get them through a lot of tricky or dangerous moves. Unlike the boys, she had to focus on finesse and moving smartly. She worked out regularly and knew she was strong, but that didn't mean she needed to be stupid if there was a better way to do something.

"I want to see how you do when the problems aren't color coated." Leslie pointed at the boulder in front of them. "Bouldering is roughly defined as climbing less than twenty feet off the ground. That doesn't mean you can't get hurt. Sure, the crash pads help, but you can get hurt if you land badly. Normally, I won't make you wear the helmet for bouldering, but it's a good habit to get into. Do you know any martial arts?"

"Aikido and Jujitsu."

"Interesting combination." She gave CJ an appraising stare. "So you know how to fall. Well, falling when you climb is the same but different. Usually, when you're getting thrown or pummeled, you have some idea it's coming and you're relatively low to the ground. When you're climbing, though, you're falling from a height, and that height could put you at a bad angle to the ground."

CJ stared at the huge boulder, looking for patterns in the rock and at the white chalk marks left by previous climbers. It looked easy but she knew looks were deceptive.

"You will fall," Leslie promised. "I'll keep you as safe as I can but you need to be aware of your surroundings and think now about how you might land."

CJ looked puzzled but didn't say anything.

"Land on your feet if you can. Bend your knees, roll if you must, but better feet than head. Let's get you on this rock. I'd like to see you start here. Study the rock and look at the hand and foot placements before you even start onto the boulder." To demonstrate, she walked up to the rock and placed her hands on it. "Feel the rock under your hands. Really feel it. It's a lot rougher than the holds at the gym. Hell on your hands." She wiggled her fingers at CJ.

Leslie's hands were long and lean. CJ had already noticed the scars on the backs of them and had been wondering how she had gotten them but as soon as she put her hands on the monzogranite rock of JT, she understood how fragile human skin was against this rock. Time to toughen up.

She looked more closely at the rock and again noted the various chalk marks left by previous climbers. She stepped closer to what appeared to be the start of the route and put her hands on the rock, getting a feel for the grip required. She looked for where to put her feet, but she wasn't seeing a starting foothold.

"Trust your shoes," said Leslie, indicating the rough lower wall. "Once you're on the wall, the placement will come with the handholds. Now show me the path you see."

CJ stared at the rock face. "I'd put my hands here and here. Then I'd push for that hold there with my left hand, shuffle my feet, here, maybe." She indicated a slight prominence. "Then over to that chalk mark with my right hand, then up to the next chalk mark there."

Leslie smiled. "Pretty good! Spot me. I'll show you the route." She reached behind her back and dipped her hands into her chalk bag, first her left and then her right, after which she shook her hands vigorously, sending a wave of chalk dust into the air. Then she spotted and climbed onto the rock, fingertips light on the wall, hips in tight, upper body leaning out slightly as she sighted further up the rock. She moved her left foot on a small nub, then reached and angled her body up and over her left foot with her right foot extended out as counterbalance. Next, her left hand went up to a hold on the boulder. She continued to climb, pausing occasionally to dip her hand in her chalk bag and shake it out. As she climbed, she pointed to each part and explained why and how she was positioning her hands.

CJ soaked it all in. As Leslie pushed over the top of the boulder, CJ began to wonder how she was going to get down. She was still staring at the top of the boulder when Leslie came around from behind the rock.

"Easy downclimb on the other side," Leslie told her. "Your turn. Take it slow and concentrate on form and placement. Remember, you want to look like you know what you're doing."

CJ nodded and chalked her hands, then placed them on the same rock features Leslie had used. She stretched herself out and thought fluid thoughts. She only got about three moves in, however, when her foot slipped and she fell backward. Leslie's hands guided her as she landed on the crash pad. She would have stumbled if Leslie hadn't been there.

"Thanks," she said, righting herself. "I see what you mean about the falls. Crash pads are good but the ground is still rocky. Glad you were there to stop me from really falling."

She had felt the strength in those hands, and the care, too. It was hard for her to rely on others. In stunt work you had to rely on your team because if you didn't, you could hurt yourself or the other members of your group. But trust didn't come easy for CJ. She had too much baggage. *Head in the game, girl.*

So she reoriented herself to the rock and started to climb again as Leslie coached from the ground. "Left foot here, turn your hips into the wall, lengthen your reach, rock your foot here, always keep your hips to the wall." This time CJ completed the climb and then did it twice more before her arms gave out.

At that point, Leslie called it a day. She squeezed CJ's bicep. "Feeling a little pumped, are we?"

CJ wiped a trickle of sweat off her forehead. She laughed as she looked down at her chalk-coated hands, knowing that she had just transferred chalk to her face and noticing for the first time a nice scrape on her right forearm. But she was happy. "That was fun."

Leslie smiled. "Yep. Let's get packed and head back to camp, get some food and then we can talk anchoring. Tomorrow we'll set a few top ropes and do some longer climbs."

"Ahhh," said CJ as she pulled off her climbing shoes.

Leslie grinned at her as she removed her own shoes. "Feels good to take them off."

"I didn't feel how tight they are when I was climbing. Hey, I noticed something on the climb."

Leslie looked up expectantly.

"I couldn't do the same moves you did, okay, well, some of them I could, but I don't have your reach."

"That's what makes every climb a puzzle for the climber," Leslie said, shoving her shoes into the duffel along with her chalk bag. "You can watch me and get a feel for the path but the path you take is your own on real rock. I've seen some incredible moves from people shorter than you that I could never manage. Tall people can't fold themselves up but they can bypass some things with their reach. Blessings and curses."

"Okay, I can see that."

"You watched me and then improvised where you didn't have the reach and made the climb your own. You're getting the feel. I'm impressed," said Leslie, shrugging into the now folded crash pad and picking up her duffel. "Ready?"

Back at the camp, CJ took off her crash pad and laid it against the camper. "I've got something for us," she said as she headed over to her truck. She opened the side door and pulled out a small cooler, which she brought back over and set on the ground before she plopped down on the chair. She opened the lid and grabbed two cold beers out of the melting ice.

"Modelo Negra?"

"Absolutely!" Leslie dropped into the chair next to CJ's. "Do you have a church key, or do I have to get back up?"

CJ reached into the cooler again, pulled out the opener, and waved it. She deftly removed the caps from the beers and passed one to Leslie.

They both settled back and drank.

"Ahhhh," Leslie said. "Nice finish to some nice climbing."

CJ drank deeply and sighed. "Good day. I think I'm going to be sore tomorrow."

"Yes, tomorrow," Leslie said. "I'd like to start by nine, if that works for you. You can have dinner with me tonight and talk anchoring. I'm having soup and grilled cheese sandwiches."

CJ was tempted but she still wasn't sure if Leslie was gay or not. She didn't want to stay and misread any signals. Her body was getting attuned to Leslie's and she was concerned that she might do something rash. Better not to tempt fate until she was sure.

"Thanks for the offer, but I'm going to head back into town. I need to make some phone calls and check on my last gig. But I'll be back by nine sharp tomorrow morning." She collected the empty bottles and stowed them back in the cooler. "I would love a grilled cheese sandwich, though. Raincheck?"

"Sure." Leslie stood and walked to the camper. "See you tomorrow." The camper's door swung shut behind her.

Well, I didn't handle that as well as I should've, did I? She wanted to trust her feelings but embarrassing herself was not something she wanted to risk. She kicked at the dirt, then headed toward her truck. Maybe Joannie or Sally, or if worse came to worst, Tom could tell her if Leslie was family.

She rubbed her cheek as she got into her truck and started driving. She was feeling the phantom pain from five years ago when she had mistakenly pulled her college roommate into a kiss and gotten a hard slap for her efforts. She and her roommate had flirted constantly and her roommate was forever touching her. She guessed she could be forgiven for misinterpreting the signs, but she could still feel that slap. And things hadn't stopped with the mistaken kiss. Her roommate had told everyone about CJ's unwanted advances. The blowback had been harsh. Even a couple of solid friends had turned on her.

It was Sally who had come through for her. Sally had known her roommate, she knew CJ, and she knew who to trust. The roommate had acted in the same flirtatious way before with people of both sexes. But history didn't lessen the fact that CJ had kissed the roommate and her kiss had been unwanted. Fortunately, she knew what *no* meant and had backed off immediately. In fact, she had moved out and moved in with Sally. While Sally's boyfriend, now husband, hadn't been pleased with the new arrangement, he wasn't unsympathetic. CJ knew when to make herself scarce and they had all become good friends. Tough times, she thought, but it was behind her now.

Before tomorrow, however, she'd need to know, one way or the other. She couldn't stop the pull of Leslie's physical presence. If Leslie wasn't a lesbian, then CJ needed to make the flirting stop. On the other hand, if Leslie was gay... She could feel her body heat up. She flipped on the AC. No cold shower for her until she was back at the hotel.

CHAPTER NINE

Leslie was frustrated. She hadn't handled that well. Watching CJ's lithe body all day and making occasional contact had only heightened her awareness. She knew CJ was gay. That much was already clear to her, but every time she made a move to get closer, CJ shied away. Was she already in a relationship? Why didn't she just come out and say she was with someone?

She pulled out the ingredients for her dinner, moving in a small circle from fridge to stove to dinette booth as she cooked. She took a beer out of the fridge and drank it slowly as the soup heated and cheese melted between the bread slices in the sizzling skillet.

There's something there, she thought. She was sure of it. But CJ was unwilling to act on the attraction between them. Just her luck. She found someone interesting, funny, intelligent, and gay and she wasn't available.

Leslie sighed. Maybe the direct approach would work. At least that would put an end to this strange situation. If CJ said she wasn't interested, they could just get back to climbing and that would be that. And then it would be awkward between them. Ugh.

She filled a bowl with soup, put the grilled cheese on a plate and carried her supper to the table. Pulling another beer out of the fridge, she stopped and put it back. Enough beer. She needed to rehydrate, and water was a better option for multiple reasons. She filled a glass and sat down at the table, still talking to herself.

Better to concentrate on teaching CJ what she needs to know to get the stunt job she wanted. Forget the personal. She pulled her copy of Randy Vogel's classic *Joshua Tree Rock Climbing Guide* closer and thumbed through the section on the Hidden Valley campground. Yes, that was the answer. Focus on the job not the person.

Her phone buzzed a few minutes later with an incoming text from Tom: *CJ called asking if you were gay*

She texted back: *What did you tell her?*

I told her to ask U.

Well, that put a different light on things. Was CJ asking because she was interested or because she was concerned by her flirting?

Curiouser and curiouser. What to do with this information?

As she contemplated the texts from Tom, her phone buzzed again. This time it was a text from Mia Todd at AZM, asking when she was coming to Boston. The last time Leslie had spoken to them, she had said she needed time to make up her mind. That was two days ago. Now they were pushing again. She felt she owed it to herself to at least visit Boston, meet the people and see what they had to offer. She'd have to book something for next week.

She texted back that she'd fly out on Tuesday. Mia texted that she'd make the reservations and send Leslie the flight information. Leslie texted back her acceptance and leaned back into the padding of the dinette booth. She had a lot to think about and a relationship would only complicate things. So CJ was off the table. Images began filling her mind. *STOP with the images already*, she ordered herself. She sighed and rubbed her face. Why did everything seem to be sexually loaded? Pulling the rock climbing guide closer, she told herself to focus on climbing. At least that felt real and solid.

The morning lights were just coming over the rocks at the campsite where Leslie was sitting in a lawn chair drinking her coffee when CJ pulled up in her truck. Her frantic phone calls the previous night had netted her exactly zip. Sally didn't know anything, nor did Joannie. That had come as a huge surprise as Joannie seemed to know everyone. The last resort was Tom. He had just laughed and said she should take it up with Leslie.

So here she was, ready for another day in close proximity to Leslie. *Just stay professional.* Aloud, she asked, "Got any extra coffee for me?"

Leslie was dressed in the same climbing pants but had on a different hoodie today. Her short hair looked mussed, as if she hadn't taken the time to do anything but run a hand through it. Her eyes were bright but wary. CJ almost walked over and dropped a kiss on her lips, which looked very kissable.

Leslie pointed at the thermos on the camper's side table, which had been lowered. "Help yourself. I left a cup out for you."

CJ spotted the cup sitting next to the thermos and poured herself some coffee.

"If you need milk or sugar, they're in the camper."

CJ took her first sip. "Black is fine." She sat in the second chair, which just happened to be next to Leslie's. "So. What's on the agenda for the day?"

Leslie took another sip of her coffee. "Old Woman."

"I'm not that old."

Leslie shook her head and grinned. "The Old Woman is a rock formation near where we were bouldering yesterday. I think there are several climbs you could do that will give you the feel and form you're looking to emulate in the film."

"Okay, do we take the crash pads today?"

"I'm going to lead climb this. You haven't done this kind of belay before but it's similar to what you've already done. In your reading, did you study traditional, or 'trad' climbing?"

"I watched a couple YouTube videos. I also watched some of the better climbers at the gym."

"The first climb I'll do to get to the top shouldn't tax me too much, but if you're not paying attention, you can pull me off the wall."

CJ frowned.

"This technique is more about letting rope out than pulling it in. If you don't give me enough rope or don't release it quickly enough, you'll pull me off the rock. I'll be taking the rope up with me. I'll place protection into cracks in the rock, clipping in as I go. It's fun, but if you fall, you fall twice the distance from the last clipped-in piece of the protection, plus any slack in the rope." Leslie left-hand pointed to a protection piece; her right showed how a fall would go from the position above the protection to that same distance below the protection. "I once fell seventy feet. Pulled my belayer right off the ground. That won't happen today, though, as this climb has a much better line for placements. And it's an easy climb for me. I don't expect to fall."

CJ contemplated this information for a minute. "Are you sure you want to trust me on this? It's your life," she said, emphasizing each word carefully.

Leslie studied her over her cup. "Yes, I trust you."

CJ felt the heat from yesterday rising again. She didn't trust many people, and to have Leslie say she trusted her not casually, but easily, had an effect on her. Maybe she could trust as well. She pushed that thought away to focus on climbing and the film.

Leslie stood and pulled a heavy sling out of a duffel resting nearby. As she hung the sling around her neck, bandoleer style, CJ noticed the various devices hanging from it.

Noticing her interest, Leslie pointed to each piece of protection as she named them. "Cams, stoppers, wire nuts. Did you pack a lunch and fluids?"

CJ nodded. She had stopped at a Stop-N-Go before entering the park.

"Okay," Leslie said in a vigorous tone. "Grab your stuff and let's go. It's a beautiful time to be on the rock." She grabbed a separate large knapsack and swung it over her shoulder. She was already wearing her harness with her climbing shoes clipped securely to it and her chalk bag was clipped around her waist.

CJ went back to her truck, picked up her equipment and followed Leslie up the trail.

They ambled up the dirt path toward the west face of The Old Woman, which was an imposing rock formation forty or fifty feet off the ground. They set up in front of a route to the right of the middle of the rock.

"The route I'm going to lead climb is called Double Cross. It's considered a classic. Normally, I'd just free climb the Northwest Chimney on this formation but I want you to see a lead climb and how it's done. I'm also going to overdo the protection so you can see how the rope movements work, how I hold my body as I place the protection, and how I clip in. This is all important for both the look and the feel of climbing to come across in the film."

Next, Leslie had CJ practice letting out the rope, pulling it taut on command, then letting out more rope. Then she simulated a fall. Doing all this work took concentration and CJ knew she really would have Leslie's life in her hands shortly. It was an exhilarating and scary feeling at the same time.

When Leslie felt that CJ was ready, she roped in, checked her own harness and then CJ's, ensuring that everything was correct. Leslie had rigged a base anchor for CJ as a precaution. She double-checked to make sure CJ's harness was clipped to it.

CJ felt nervous. This was stuff she needed to learn but Leslie was moving so fast.

"You got this," Leslie said, as if CJ would be doing the climbing and not her. "Watch and learn. You'll clean, which means you'll remove each piece as you climb up." She handed CJ a smooth, flat piece of metal that had an edge about six inches long on a tether and a carabiner for clipping it to her belt.

"I don't expect any of the pieces to be hard to remove but take this in case you have a problem."

Instructions given, Leslie studied the rock for a moment and then stepped up to the route. She pulled toward the first section to place her first protection device in the crack. Then she set her feet wide apart, held her hips close to the wall and raised her left hand to grip a monzogranite edge. She selected a small cam with her right hand, unclipped it from her belt and set the webbing between her teeth so she could reposition her hand to the cam grip, deftly work the cam action, and slide the piece into position in the crevice. She released the cam, which opened as she released it. She gave it a good tug before she pulled on the rope below her, again using her teeth as a separate appendage to hold the rope and reach to pull up more rope, which she clipped into the carabiner attached to the webbing and the cam. Each protection placement would hold her weight in the event of a fall but could also easily be removed by the second climber as they were belayed from above by the first climber.

It was all so smooth and fluid. Practiced, even. CJ watched Leslie's motions carefully as she minded the rope, letting it out, then pulling the extra back as Leslie worked her way up the rock face.

Near the top of the climb, Leslie shifted her weight to her left foot before carefully reaching for the small, pencil-fine ridge of granite above her. Grasping the rough rock with two fingers and a thumb, she brought her right foot level to her hip and placed it over a small fissure in the rock wall. She rocked her hip over her right foot and gracefully straightened her knee. The ledge was shoulder height. She found an outcropping and pulled herself up. The Hidden Valley campsite lay before her. The early morning camp sounds played against birdsong. The sky was clear and the cool breeze ruffled her hair.

Now she peered over the ledge at the woman standing forty feet below her. "Give me some slack," she called. "I'll set up an anchor and then it's your turn." She rummaged through the equipment harness she had lugged up with her and quickly placed three protection pieces. She set a nylon strap and carabiners in an equalized grouping so no one piece would take more stress than the others. Setting two more pieces, she created an anchor for herself, then rechecked all the anchors, tied herself to the second anchor, and clipped the rope through the carabiners of the equalized three pieces. A final sharp tug on the rope completed her assessment of the situation.

"Belay off," she called down. "When you're ready to climb, let me know."

CJ released her grip on the belay. She unclipped the ATC, pulled the rope free and stowed the ATC on her belt. Then she quickly tied herself in with the figure-eight knot and tied the protective double knot. Looking up at Leslie, she called, "On belay?"

Leslie quickly pulled in the rope until she felt the tension in the line. "Belay on."

As CJ climbed, Leslie kept the line taut. CJ was new to climbing, so climbing and cleaning would be a challenge for her, but Leslie wanted her to understand the process and learn how to really center herself as she climbed. Having to do multiple things would ensure that she found that balance in herself.

It was slow work, but CJ worked her way steadily up the path Leslie had taken. She seemed to be trying to mimic the stances Leslie had taken at each location, trying to settle herself into those confident placements. Keeping her hips close to the wall, she chalked her hands repeatedly. She pulled all of the pieces from the cracks as she climbed and clipped them to her harness loops. It was slow going but the taut rope seemed to give her confidence that she wouldn't fall. Finally, breathing heavily, she pulled herself over the top.

"Nicely done," Leslie said, smiling broadly. "Nicely done. I didn't do half so well the first time I did what you just did."

CJ grinned back at her. "Wow! That. Was. Awesome!" She impulsively hugged Leslie, whose hands were still on the ropes holding her belay.

"Hey, wait until you're anchored in up here," Leslie told her. "I'd like to hug you back, but my hands are a little busy here making sure you stay safe."

CJ blushed and tried to back up. The tight belay stopped her from falling off the edge of the cliff face. She quickly regained her footing and stepped to a more protected spot on the top of the rock.

The hug had felt good, and Leslie would have liked to return it with feeling, but she wasn't about to do something as stupid as take her hands off the line without CJ being properly tied in the anchor she'd set—or at least farther from the edge. It was relatively safe on the top of the rock, but she knew how easy it was to make a misstep.

CJ's inscrutable mask had reappeared. Leslie knew the moment was gone. That was too bad. CJ's hug had been warm and spontaneous.

"Sorry," CJ said. "I don't know what came over me. I guess… well, the climb made me feel so alive."

"It makes me feel the same way. Look around. It's beautiful up here."

CJ stepped further up on The Old Woman and scanned the area.

"Wow, it's stunning with all the light and shadows on the rocks. You can see the campsite too," she said, shielding her eyes. Then she suddenly pointed. "A hawk!"

"I love it here," Leslie said, noticing the way the breeze ruffled CJ's hair and a streak of chalk on her face. It gave her a rakish look.

They stood close together. Leslie still had her on belay.

"Off belay?" CJ asked. "Is that okay up here?"

"As long as you feel stable and secure," Leslie said. "I'd like to switch over to a top rope configuration now if you feel comfortable enough without being tied into an anchor."

"I'm good."

"Okay, off belay, then." Leslie unclipped the rope but kept it in hand. "Go ahead and untie from the rope. We're both going to rappel down and then we'll do the harder climb next to the one you just completed."

"Can you explain the anchoring setup?"

Leslie explained the three-point system, balancing the lines against the strain and line wear patterns. As Leslie showed CJ the anchor layout and explained the intricacies, their shoulders bumped a few times. CJ moved back immediately but then focused on the conversation again and leaned in closer to the anchor, only to bump into Leslie again. The third time it happened, Leslie laughed and said, "I didn't know anchoring was so interesting, although I know it can be hazardous if it's improperly set."

CJ blushed.

"Later," Leslie said, choosing to ignore CJ's reaction. "I'll have you set up some anchors in different situations. That will come in really handy for you, both in climbing and any other roping setup you need to do. Rope management is really important." Matching actions to her words, she laid out the anchor and ropes to support the rappel. "You've rappelled before, haven't you?"

"A few times but never quite like this." CJ looked down the line of the rope at the edge of The Old Woman. "I've gone off a building. It was a fake building about twenty feet tall in a studio surrounded by green screen. Nothing like this."

"Same basic premise but you have to contend with walls that aren't smooth and rocks and other hazards behind you. This isn't the gym. No big bounces, just slow and easy, in control. Mind the rope and your hands. Do you want me to go first?"

Leslie waited patiently for a response. She could tell that CJ was hesitant and didn't want to push her. Rappelling wasn't easy for everyone.

"I'll go," CJ said as she stepped up and took both sides of the rope and slipped them through her ATC. Then she clipped the setup to her harness with a locking carabiner. With her left hand on the rope above the ATC and her right on the rope below the ATC, she started to let rope out and backed toward the edge.

Leslie stopped her before she could walk backward off the cliff. She checked CJ's setup and squeezed her forearm. "You've got this. Slow and easy, it's not a race. Watch the landing. See you at the bottom. Let me know when you're off rope."

CJ nodded and carefully released the rope and stepped back off the cliff face. Halfway down it became smoother and part of her wanted to leap and bounce her way down. She bobbled the landing, trying to step down without giving herself enough rope, then stumbling a little when she did. She stepped back and looked up to see Leslie watching her from the top. CJ waved and released herself from the rope.

"Rope is yours," she called up.

Leslie clipped in so fast she was on the ground before CJ had time to take a few more steps backward to clear a path for her. Leslie made it look so much easier. But that was what practice brought.

Leslie pointed to the right of the route they had just completed. "This route is much harder than the one we just did. I don't expect you to complete this but the techniques on this one will help you."

CJ looked up at the newer expanse of rock. The friendly crack that she had used so easily wasn't available here. She wasn't sure how climbing on something impossible was going to teach her anything. She turned to Leslie to tell her that and saw that Leslie couldn't keep a serious face.

Leslie burst out laughing. "You should have seen your face."

CJ frowned. She noticed some nearby climbers looking over their way, so she waved at them and turned back to Leslie. "Very funny."

"Sorry, I couldn't resist, and you did say you wanted to be an expert climber," she waved at the climb. "This climb, Route 499, is rated a 5.11b. It would be a challenge for me and I am an expert." She laughed again but this time it seemed to be with joy rather than at CJ's expense. "You get to work on Double Cross until you feel comfortable. It has many of the elements you'll need to know. I'm going to correct your stance, your finger holds, your body placement. You're going to get sick of this climb. And me."

CJ tied in and they got to work. After three hours, CJ's fingers were a mess, rubbed raw and stiff. Her arms were so pumped she felt like they were made of concrete, even though on the last run she had felt moments of fluid grace, like she was one with the rock and that they were working together.

Leslie hadn't made a single comment on the last run. CJ had hit every mark, working through the route as if she owned it. Only at the very top had she felt a tremor in her grip.

CJ was looking to step onto the rock again when Leslie called a halt to the exercise.

"Enough," she said. "The last run looked really good. But you're done. Or at least your arms are."

CJ sighed and plopped down on a nearby rock, heedless of the dirt.

"How do you feel?" Leslie asked. "Do you feel the difference in your climbing yet?"

CJ nodded. She was definitely tired but she was also feeling like she was making progress.

"Let's eat and then I get a run at Route 499. Watching you climb has made me jealous."

After cleaning their hands using biodegradable suds, they sat down and ate their sandwiches and fruit. CJ was surprised at how hungry she was. Up on the rock, she hadn't paid any attention to her stomach, but now that she was eating, she wished she'd made two sandwiches.

They finished quickly and Leslie tied in and stepped up to climb. Standing in front of the new route, she slowly worked her hands, lining up her moves as if she were choreographing a dance she would perform. CJ was mesmerized by her intensity and concentration as she moved through the steps she would take as she climbed. Leslie turned. "Climbing?"

"Climb on," CJ replied.

The sequence Leslie had mimed was almost an exact duplicate of the moves she made as she climbed the route. It was far more intricate and subtle than the route CJ had worked. CJ couldn't even see many of the holds from her position on the ground. It was a beautiful climb with a few momentary pauses as Leslie reached behind her back for her chalk bag to reduce the sweat on her fingertips or give her hands and arms a rest.

When she reached the top, she called down, "I'm going to the top to pull down the anchor. I'll let you know when I'm off rope. I'll use an existing rappel anchor to lower myself from the other side."

CJ shouted up an acknowledgment and let out rope as Leslie crested the top of The Old Woman.

The rest of the afternoon was taken up with different bouldering routes and more lessons in anchor setting. By four o'clock, CJ was worn out.

Leslie led the way back to the campsite. "Beer?"

CJ could only nod as she sat down carefully in the lawn chair.

Leslie got the beers and handed one to her. They polished them off quickly and CJ went for a second round for them both.

"You did well today," Leslie said, sipping the second beer more slowly.

"But will it be enough? I have to get this job."

"Why? Why is this so important?"

CJ didn't know if it was the exhaustion, the second beer, or the real concern in Leslie's voice, but she felt she owed Leslie an explanation. "My parents are both in the film business," she paused, taking another swallow, "I don't want their help. I need to do this on my own." She looked down at the now empty beer bottle in her hand. "They want to help. Pave the way for me. They think I have the looks to be an actor and they want me to be one."

Leslie nodded but didn't say anything.

"I don't want to be an actor. I've seen what it does to people." She finished her beer and waved the empty bottle at Leslie as she stood up. "Another one?"

Leslie shook her head.

CJ pulled another beer out of the cooler. "I don't need this but it'll help me finish this story. My brother is an actor. A successful actor on a successful sitcom." She shook her head. "It's not my thing to be recognized wherever I go and fawned over. But I love being on set and working with the crew. I love the excitement of seeing the planning and execution of a successful stunt." She sat back down in the chair. "I want to do great stunts. Learn from the best. Then be the one that creates the next generation of those stunts for film and TV." She leaned her head back and stared into the west, where the sun was beginning to set behind the local rocks. The sky was starting to get a beautiful purple cast. "I want to do it my way and on my own without their help. I want my success to be my own."

They were silent for a while, listening to the hum of the campground as other climbers and hikers returned from their day's activities. A nearby campsite had a classic rock station playing. They sat quietly as Otis Redding's "Sitting on the Dock of the Bay" played. When the next song came up, CJ stood and shuffled her feet to the music, slowly swaying to the tune as Leon Redbone played "Come and Get Your Love," brought back to popularity as the opening song from *Guardians of the Galaxy*.

She turned and saw Leslie watching her. She danced over and pulled Leslie to her feet. "Dance with me."

Leslie pulled CJ close and kissed her. Then she quickly turned away. "Let me make you something to eat to absorb some of that alcohol," she called over her shoulder as she entered the camper.

CJ froze, then raised one hand and touched her lips. Her brain was indeed starting to feel the effects of the alcohol. That had been a little more than a friendly peck. She had her answer: Leslie was family. She smiled and as the next song came on, she kept dancing.

CHAPTER TEN

Leslie wasn't sure if the kiss had been a good idea. CJ had looked so sad and then sexy as she danced. The second beer had hit her system and it had seemed like a good idea when she did it. Oh well, done was done. She opened cabinets and pulled out spaghetti and sauce. As she fixed dinner, she thought back to what CJ had told her. She could understand wanting to do things for yourself, but it was a mistake to think your success was only your own. There were always those who helped you along the way. She hoped she could help CJ realize her dream, or at least take a step along the path.

With dinner ready, she opened the camper door to find CJ still dancing to the tunes coming from the radio in the nearby camp. "Come in," she called from the doorway. "It's getting cold."

CJ, a Modela Negra in one hand, stumbled as she turned to Leslie. She had been drinking Modela Special when Leslie had gone in to make dinner. Now she sashayed over to Leslie and ran a hand along her hip and went into the camper. Leslie snagged the beer as she went by.

CJ sat at the dinette and gazed at the salad and spaghetti before her. "Looks great," she said, a slight slur in her voice. The slur wouldn't have been noticeable if Leslie hadn't known how many beers she'd had.

She slid in the other side of the dinette. "Dig in. You did some hard work today."

CJ made appropriate happy noises as she ate. When she had polished off a second plate of spaghetti, she sighed and put her head back on the edge of the plush seat. "I should head back to the hotel."

"Nope."

CJ sat up and eyed Leslie.

"You've had a least four beers," said Leslie, looking at her watch. "That means you can go back slowly at midnight and make sure you don't hit any wildlife. Or you can sleep here." For emphasis, she waved CJ's truck keys at her.

CJ started to object but the look in Leslie's eyes stopped her. "I guess I'll be staying here," she said. "I keep some spare clothes in the truck but you'll have to spot me a toothbrush."

"Tom has spares of all sorts of toiletries in this camper. I think he thinks the world is going to be invaded like in *Independence Day*, and this is his RV for the desert trek to Area 51."

CJ laughed. "Since I don't get to leave, can I have another beer? Or am I cut off?"

"It's up to you, but we have another significant day of climbing tomorrow and I don't know if you want to climb hung-over."

"Right. Water, then."

Leslie pointed to the cabinet with the glasses. CJ pulled a glass down, then poured water into it from the water jug on the counter.

"It's too early for bed," CJ said. "So…what do you do in JT at night?"

"Tom has a collection of movies you can check out," Leslie replied, not taking the bait, "but I like to go out and look at the stars. Joshua Tree National Park is considered a dark sky location. It's not as great as some places I've been to, and the Palm Springs lights seem to get more intense every year. Ultimately that could wreck JT's sky. Still, it's dark enough, especially in the campsites that have rocks to the south blocking the stray Palm Springs light pollution. You get a great view of the night sky."

"Sounds great."

Leslie walked to the back of the camper and pulled out a heavy jacket and a blanket. "You may want to wear something heavier or you can borrow one of Tom's jackets if you need to. Like I said, he has spare everything in this RV. The temperature drops quickly in the desert."

"I've got a coat in the truck."

Leslie tossed CJ her keys and was slightly surprised to see CJ snag them in midair. Maybe she wasn't as inebriated as Leslie thought she was.

Leslie slipped on her coat and waited as CJ got her stuff from her truck. The temperature had dropped about twenty degrees since they had entered the camper. Without the sunlight, the desert cooled off quickly.

CJ shrugged into her jacket and pulled a small duffel from the truck.

She set the bag inside the camper and followed Leslie, who walked toward the trailhead using the moon to light the way. Leslie found a quiet spot behind some boulders that blocked the light and most of the sounds from the other campsites. She laid the blanket on the ground and sat down, gesturing at CJ to do the same. Leslie leaned back and looked up at the sky. She contemplated the Milky Way, which spread in a distinct path across the sky above the desert.

After a minute, CJ lay down next to her, but without touching her. She could feel the small rocks and twigs under the blanket, but she was comfortable enough. Then she looked up at the night sky and forgot about the rocks. "Wow," she said. "I don't think I've seen the Milky Way this clearly since I was a kid."

Leslie just gazed at the sky.

They lay there for a while, watching the sky, a radio playing and an occasional laugh or yell from a nearby campsite. CJ was starting to doze when Leslie grabbed her hand and said, "Did you see the shooting star?"

CJ's eyes popped open. She turned to Leslie, who was still watching the sky but hadn't let go of her hand. There was little light available from the campsite to see by, but CJ could make out Leslie's face as she watched the starry sky. She looked happy and relaxed.

Propping herself up on her elbow, CJ leaned over and kissed her. Leslie's lips were soft yet firm. Her arms came around CJ and pulled her closer. CJ relaxed into the kiss and their tongues' dance. Eventually, CJ came up for breath, her heart racing. What had started out simple felt like a lot more.

Leslie reached up and caressed CJ's cheek. "Took you long enough," she said with a smile in her voice. Her hand moved to the back of CJ's neck and pulled her back down for another kiss.

The second kiss was soft and relaxed. When it ended, they were both out of breath, Leslie's hands were in CJ's hair, and CJ was holding herself up with already tired arms. She rolled back to her side of the blanket.

"I guess I'm a slow learner," she sighed. "But I can learn." She rolled to her side and, with her head propped on her hand said, "You're beautiful, smart, sexy, confident. I didn't know if you were gay or just a big flirt."

"Well I don't normally flirt at all. Just ask my friend Carrie. She says I'm dull, dull, dull." Leslie mimicked a young woman's voice. "She's been trying to set me up with a new Zero G route setter. I've been ignoring her."

CJ chuckled. "You could have fooled me. I tried to find out if you were gay from my sources. Nothing."

"Tom texted me last night."

"That snot."

"He's a good friend. He texted that you'd asked if I was gay. I wasn't sure what to make of that. Did you want me to be or were you afraid that I was?"

CJ laughed. "I've had issues in the past," she paused and then added, "I didn't want to move on you if you weren't available."

She felt Leslie shift next to her.

"You are available, aren't you? You're not in a relationship with the route setter?"

"I'm safe from the route setter but I'm traveling to Boston to check out a job opportunity."

"Boston. Why Boston?"

"Long story. I'm going out Tuesday to talk to the company directors and see if I want to work there. I'll also be checking out the area to see where I might want to live." She sighed and locked her fingers together and put her hands behind her head.

"I thought your career was climbing," CJ said as she reached out to brush a strand of hair back from Leslie's forehead.

Leslie smiled. "It's what I love but it doesn't pay the bills. I'm still paying off college debt. No, I'm a computer programmer. I design the graphics for businesses and business websites."

"I'll have to add creative to my list for you."

Abruptly, Leslie scrambled to her feet. She reached down, took CJ's hand and pulled her to her feet. "Let's head back. I need sleep, even if you don't."

They walked back to the camper in silence. Leslie had brought a flashlight so they found their way quietly through the jumble of rocks without stumbling. The short walk ended quickly and they entered the camper.

"You can sleep on the ledge over the driver's seat," Leslie said, pointing to the front of the camper. "There's a double-size mattress. I'll give you first shot at the bathroom. It's small. You can take a shower but keep it very short. Limited water and all." She turned away and busied herself with the dirty dishes they had left on the dinette.

CJ wasn't quite sure what had happened. She grabbed her bag from where she had tossed it just inside the door. Taking it to the dinette seat by the bunk area, she pulled out a T-shirt, a towel and her bag of toiletries. She squeezed past Leslie, who was standing at the sink. Leslie didn't comment, and CJ headed back to the small bathroom.

Leslie was sitting on the queen bed when CJ came out of the bathroom fifteen minutes later. She had taken a brief shower and was still toweling her hair dry when she noticed Leslie watching her.

"You asked if I'm available," Leslie began, smoothing out imaginary wrinkles in the quilt covering the bed.

CJ nodded.

"I don't know if I'm available. If I want to continue with my current job, I'll have to move to Boston. Otherwise, I have to find a new job in LA which could be challenging. They really want me in Boston, and it's a great opportunity that would solve so many of my financial problems."

CJ sat down on the edge of the bed and put her hand over Leslie's, stopping its ceaseless movement.

"Change is hard."

Leslie linked their fingers. "I'm not up for one-night stands and you're one more reason not to go to Boston. But I made a commitment to go see what they have to offer. I'm going to take it seriously."

After giving Leslie's hand a squeeze, CJ climbed off the bed. "I understand. Get some sleep. A rested mind works better than a tired one."

Leslie looked like she wanted to reach for her, but didn't. She nodded her thanks at CJ's understanding, then stood up and went into the bathroom.

CJ draped her wet towel over the back of the passenger seat, turned off the camper's overhead light, and climbed onto the front cabin bunk. It wasn't quite a double bed. She had no idea when Leslie had put bedding up there, but she found a couple of top sheets, a nice quilt, and a pillow. She layered the bedding to suit herself and crawled under the covers. It was comfortable, even with the roof so close.

She turned on her side, stared out the dome at the front of the RV and began thinking about the day. Her muscles were tired and her fingers were raw. The JT rock was hard on the hands. She thought about the feelings she was starting to have for Leslie. Their kisses felt so right but she also understood Leslie's hesitation.

She rolled over as Leslie came out of the bathroom. The light from the bathroom backlit her lean, long-legged form through the thin T-shirt she wore. With that image in her mind, CJ wondered how she was going to sleep.

Leslie looked up and caught CJ's eyes. "Sleep well," she said as she turned off the bathroom light and crawled into her own bed.

CHAPTER ELEVEN

CJ woke to the sounds of Leslie cooking breakfast. The smell of pancakes and eggs was enticing. She noticed Leslie was already dressed in another pair of worn climbing pants and a hoodie, though her small feet were bare, her toes curling and uncurling as she stirred the scrambled eggs in the pan.

CJ jumped down from the bunk. Her muscles were sore and stiff as she stretched her body. As she stepped past Leslie to get to the bathroom, Leslie reached out and patted her ass. CJ turned abruptly and Leslie pulled her into a kiss. CJ's nipples hardened as Leslie's tongue touched hers. Then Leslie released her as quickly as she had grabbed her.

"Morning."

"Morning," CJ mumbled back, still unsteady from the kiss. She would have stayed right where she was but she needed the comfort of the bathroom so she continued to the back of the RV. When she returned, Leslie had set two plates of food on the dinette. CJ slid into the booth and smiled at Leslie. She was a little more awake after her morning ablutions.

"I could get used to this," CJ said, smiling as Leslie filled her coffee cup.

"Fat chance. I rarely cook and my repertoire is very limited. Let me see your hands." She held out her hands toward CJ.

The non sequitur surprised CJ, but she placed her hands carefully in Leslie's. Her fingers were sore and she felt as if she'd lost enough layers of skin that she could pull off a heist and not leave fingerprints.

Leslie tested the pad of each of CJ's fingers, then checked for cuts and scrapes on her palms and the backs of her hands. "Not too bad," she said. "I think we should tape your fingers today and try some bigger crack climbing where you'll be wedging your whole hand, and potentially your whole body into the cracks."

"Sounds good," CJ said through a mouthful of egg.

They spent the rest of the day alternating between climbing and discussions of climbing. Leslie explained why certain moves worked better than others and how visually some moves that didn't work at all would film well. There was a lot of laughter.

As they moved to different locations, Leslie would stop and talk with the other climbers in the area, getting Beta on various climbs and trails. Beta, Leslie explained, was the term climbers used for discussing information and techniques used on various climbs. Climbing was very individual but it was also communal. Climbers were a community of people who loved solving problems that tested both the mind and the body. Like any sport, she said, the participants loved to share information and to challenge each other. But climbing wasn't like football, baseball or even gymnastics. There were no big displays after a success, only a quiet nod or maybe a fist bump that signaled a major accomplishment. Success was personal.

While CJ enjoyed Leslie's easy confidence as they moved from climb to climb, she was learning more about the spirit of climbing as she watched Leslie talk with the other climbers. Leslie would just stop and gaze at the rock for long minutes, saying nothing, before turning and walking quietly to the next rock face. She could tell this was Leslie's world.

As the day on the rocks ended, they came back to the camper. CJ pulled Leslie into her arms and kissed her, first tenderly and then with more passion.

"Dare greatly," she said against Leslie's lips.

Leslie pulled back, looked closely into CJ's eyes, and nodded.

They spent the next few hours in an embrace, sharing, caressing, pushing each other to greater depths of sexual tension and release, getting up only for food and drink. Sleeping and waking in each other's arms, enjoying the feel and comfort of their shared warmth in the chilly camper.

The next morning, as the light from the rising sun was just hitting the camper, CJ received a text from Joannie: *where R U?*

She had gotten up to use the bathroom as she checked her phone. She had not canceled her reservation at the hotel in Yucca Valley. Her stuff was still there and she knew the hotel was probably also wondering where she was. She'd need to take a drive back into Yucca Valley to clear out her stuff and finalize her bill.

She looked at Leslie, who was starting to wake with the morning light. She was thinking about climbing into bed for some morning sex when a second text from Joannie came through: *UR parents R looking 4 U.*

CJ sighed and texted Joannie back: *in JT with Leslie.*

Joannie replied, *OOOOOOOH*

I'll call U from hotel 2 hrs

CJ smiled and looked up. Leslie was watching her. "Joannie," she said, nodding at her phone. "My roommate," she added, noticing Leslie's raised eyebrows. "We share a condo in the city. We aren't a couple, or we aren't anymore. We found we were better friends than lovers. I'm single...or was single. Now I'm not sure." CJ recognized that she was babbling and shut up before she could dig a bigger hole.

"Well," Leslie finally said, "I'm not going to be dating anyone else until we figure out our status."

CJ leaned over and kissed her but moved out of reach before Leslie could pull her down in the warm bed.

"Joannie says my parents are looking for me. That never bodes well for anyone. I've got to check in with her. I also need to check out of the hotel. If you're okay, I'd like to stay here with you for the next few days."

Leslie's smile was all she needed to know she'd made the right choice.

CJ found her clothes and got dressed while Leslie pulled out cereal and milk for breakfast. They ate in companionable silence.

"I'll be back in time for lunch. I'll let you know if there's a problem."

They shared a long kiss before CJ broke it off and headed for her truck. She hated that she had to leave. It was a beautiful, crisp morning in Joshua Tree and between climbing and exploring the secrets of Leslie's body, she just didn't want to be doing anything else.

CHAPTER TWELVE

CJ called Joannie as soon as she left the park. Joannie didn't know anything other than her parents were looking for her and wanted to know if she had a new girlfriend. That must be, CJ thought, why her dad had called Joannie and not her. Information. Joannie was easy to get information out of, especially if you had information to trade.

She reached the hotel, packed and checked out. Then, sitting in her truck in front of the hotel, she called her dad.

"Hey, CJ," he said. "Where are you?"

"Joshua Tree. What's up? Why the call to Joannie?"

"Your mom and I want to know what you're doing for the holidays."

"So why call Joannie?"

She could hear the sound of people talking in the background as her dad answered, "We like Joannie. So are you coming for Thanksgiving? Bringing anyone with you?"

"I'll be there," CJ replied, then added after a brief pause, "I may have a friend with me."

"Good, good. Your mom and I want to see you. Jason will be here. And Cheryl with her family."

Thinking of her brother being there made her tense. Every time her brother was there, her parents were always pointing out his successful acting career and trying to get her to go in that direction.

As if hearing her thoughts, her dad added, "I saw Eddie McGinty a couple of days ago, and he said he'd be happy to have you read for that part I was telling you about. You should give him a call."

CJ gritted her teeth and said as pleasantly as she could manage, "I'm not acting these days, Dad, I'm working on stunts."

"You should give him a call," he said, ignoring her statement. "Gotta run. Your mom and I are working out the money for a new film. Talk to you later. We'll expect you and your friend by two o'clock." And he hung up.

CJ stared at the phone. She loved her dad, but he never seemed to listen to her or care about what she wanted. But maybe she didn't give him enough credit. He'd always been inspired by her successes but then he immediately turned and pushed her in ways she didn't want to go. She shook her head. It was so frustrating and sometimes infuriating.

She was headed to the local store when her phone rang. She hit the answer key on her steering wheel and Brad Carter's voice came over the speaker.

"Hey, CJ," he said. "Where are you?"

"I'm just outside of Joshua Tree National Park."

"Working on your climbing? Excellent. But I need you in LA. Scheduling got moved up, and I need to choreograph some scenes. I need you here today. When can you get to the lot?"

CJ frowned. "I thought you didn't need me until Monday."

"Jack sprained his ankle at Zero G," Brad said. "I need you here now. If you want the job, I need you here by one o'clock this afternoon. Yes or no?"

"On my way. See you at one, Sound Stage 3?"

"Yep," Brad said just before he hung up.

CJ had just pulled into the grocery store lot. *Damn.* She wasn't going to get back to Leslie today but it looked like she was going to get her chance with Brad. She tried to call Leslie but either the service wasn't working well or Leslie wasn't picking up. So, she finally left a voice mail and then a text. *Have to go back to LA. Jack sprained his ankle & Brad wants me on the lot today. Will call U later*

CJ hesitated and then sent another text: *miss U already*

She waited a few minutes but didn't see a reply, so she turned out of the parking lot and headed for Los Angeles.

Leslie heard her phone buzz as she was completing a boulder run. She had joined some local climbers and had been working the boulder problem with them all morning. It had been a fun and relaxing day, though she missed working with CJ and was looking forward to her return.

What they had shared last night had been magical but that didn't change the choices in front of both of them. "Dare greatly," CJ had said. Leslie didn't know if she was referencing the book of that title by Brené Brown or the quote from Theodore Roosevelt that Brown's book took its title from.

Leslie had often said "Dare greatly" whenever she wanted to try something new and others had tried to force her back into a box of their own construction. That was what had taken her to Nationals. It had been a dare by a friend who had said that she wasn't willing to take the risk to compete and challenge herself against the nation's best climbers in a public arena. A dare that had ended up giving Leslie her first broken heart. Now she found it interesting that CJ had used those same words to her last night.

Checking her phone, she read CJ's text.

Well, that was that. The rest of the week was her own. What did she want to do with it? It was just work. She knew CJ wasn't abandoning her, but it sure felt that way. She had gone in eyes wide open. CJ had told her what her goals were and Leslie didn't necessarily fit. CJ had already paid for her time so she could climb or leave. Her choice.

"Hey, Leslie," said Adam. "You going to join us on Gnarl Bait?"

The group she was working with were packing up to head to the next site. Adam and his friends had welcomed her in with easy, companionable grace. She had watched for a while to see how they were attacking the problem and listened to their descriptions and plans. During a pause in their climbing, she had stepped up and begun the route herself. At first the group was surprised, but as she worked through the problem, solving issues that they'd had, they had welcomed her and included her in their conversation and easy banter. This was what she liked so much about climbing: the simple inclusion.

"Sounds good," Leslie replied. "Let me answer this text and I'll follow you."

Good luck

Today she would climb and get her balance back. Tomorrow could wait. Grabbing her gear and crash pad, she followed Adam and his friends.

CHAPTER THIRTEEN

CJ got to the studio at twelve forty-five and slipped into Sound Stage 3. The team was already hard at work. Craftspeople worked on the various sets that would shape the bulk of the film's scenes. Jerry Smytheson and Brad were gesturing and commenting with the set designers on one of the sets. CJ approached, not interrupting the flow of comments and questions.

Brad nodded at her but continued to answer Jerry's question. "Yes, we can set that up for you." He glanced at CJ. "CJ is our climbing expert. She'll make sure that Brendon and Susan look great." Then he turned, opening the circle to include her.

CJ knew she wasn't the expert but she wasn't going to contradict Brad. She shook Jerry's hand.

Jerry waved at the set designer. "Do you know Gloria?"

CJ nodded and shook hands with Gloria. "Nice to see you again."

"Well," said Jerry, "I'll leave you to work out the details. I'd like a working layout and step-by-step stunt walkthrough by Monday."

As Jerry left with Gloria and his assistants, Brad nodded, turned to CJ, and checked his watch. "I actually didn't think you'd make the one p.m. cutoff I gave you. I guess you're serious. Eddie said you weren't but he's trying to get you to go over to the bright side." He laughed at his own joke. CJ forced a smile and tried not to roll her eyes as she remembered her dad telling her that Eddie McGinty had a part for her in his next film. Then he walked to a table strewn with photographs of various famous rock faces. "Did you hear what Jerry wants?"

"Most of it," she said, looking at the photos. "Have they picked a location yet?"

"We're going with Joshua Tree. Jerry wants to go local and show off the crazy rock formations, the colors of the area, the beautiful night skies. He says El Cap is way overdone." He picked up a stack of glossy photos and handed them to her. "These are the ones that Jerry thinks have potential. Pare it down to three and give me a plan of how you'd set it up. What the moves for the climb are. You'll have Sam and Bonnie to help you with the camera angles." He looked her in the eye. "And you'll be doing all the climbing. Jack and Jill are out."

CJ could feel her face freeze. She wasn't good enough to do the climbs she knew Jerry wanted. "Can I bring in outside help for the climbs?" she asked. "I have someone who can make this look incredible."

"I thought you were an expert climber," Brad said, putting his hand out for the photos.

CJ didn't give them to him. "I can do this. However, different climbs require different skills and I have someone who's the full package."

He looked at her thoughtfully. "Well, put your team together and get me a plan."

"You'll have it." She stuffed the photos into her messenger bag. As she turned toward the door, she texted Leslie.

CJ glanced up from Leslie's climbing guidebook and smiled when Leslie entered the RV, crash pad and duffel in hand. She quickly moved from the dinette to Leslie. Seeing the phone in Leslie's hand, she grimaced. As she reached for her, Leslie stepped back, her expression neutral.

"Guess you didn't get my texts," CJ said.

"Not until I saw your truck." Leslie put down her crash pad and divested herself of the rest of her gear. "So you need my help. The texts didn't seem to be very specific."

"Let me get you a beer and I'll explain," CJ said, going to the small fridge. "I brought up some more food, water, and beer."

Leslie accepted the beer but did not sit at the dinette. As CJ pulled a second beer from the fridge, she noted Leslie's watchful eyes on her.

"I need your help," CJ said, uncapping her beer. "Brad gave me the job but he thinks I can do all the climbing." She shook her head. "You and I both know I can't. I need you to do the climbing."

Not saying a word, Leslie took a sip of her beer and started putting away her gear.

"You'll get stunt pay. It's good money."

Leslie still didn't answer.

"I have to have a detailed plan, including climbing details, by Monday."

Leslie examined the photographs of some of the classic Joshua Tree rock formations. "You have me through Sunday. I fly to Boston on Tuesday."

CJ slumped back in the booth. She had half of what she needed. She knew that with Leslie's help, Sam, Bonnie, and she could put together a great plan. But she needed the whole package.

"When are you back from Boston?" she asked, reaching for Leslie's hand again.

But Leslie put her hands in her lap. "Friday," she said flatly.

CJ could read the tension in her body. "What's wrong?"

Leslie reached for her beer, drank half of it, and then set it down with a thud. "Nothing." She reached for the photos. "Nothing at all." She held up one photo. "This is Timbuktu Towers and around the corner, the Ivory Tower. Great climbing in Wonderland." She pointed to another photo. "This is Pillars of Pain Tower two at Turtle Rock. That's in Hidden Valley. Climbing isn't as good but it's photogenic."

When CJ didn't comment, Leslie tapped another photo lying near CJ's elbow. "Patagonia Pile. Interesting climbing on the East Face. Photogenic from the west face." Pulling another photo from the stack, she said, "Astro Dome. Great climbing. Looks like big wall climbing. This is in Wonderland, too."

CJ was sorting the photos as Leslie talked. It looked like Wonderland would be the area of choice. It had a little of everything. "I like Ivory Tower and Astro Dome," she said, moving those photos to the center of the table. She reached over and took Leslie's hands. "I appreciate this."

"You paid for my guiding services and expertise." She pulled her hands free and stood. "I need dinner."

CJ pointed to some takeout containers on the counter. "I brought some enchiladas from a restaurant just outside the park. I can put them in a dish and warm them in the oven." She smiled what she hoped was a charming smile. "My cooking repertoire is limited to takeout."

Leslie's laugh was more of a snort, though it showed genuine amusement.

CJ stood and moved toward Leslie. "I missed climbing with you today."

But Leslie's hand came up. "Don't. You came back for work, not for me. Or rather, not for me personally, but for what I can help you with."

CJ couldn't argue with that. She had come back for Leslie's help. That didn't mean she didn't want Leslie, too, but she didn't push. She didn't understand Leslie's feelings but she needed to work her past them. In her head, she repeated that she wanted the whole package. "Well," she said, reaching for the towel she had been using as an oven mitt, "Let me get dinner ready. You go clean up and relax. I got this."

As Leslie turned away, CJ knew this was not the end of the conversation. They'd have to settle it before bed tonight. She had plans for that, too.

Leslie grabbed some clean clothes and headed for the bathroom. She had been so excited to see CJ's truck behind the camper...until she read the texts. CJ needed her expertise. She should be thrilled to get paid for doing something she loved. But coming from CJ after the night they shared, this seemed like a setback. Even though she believed CJ wasn't just using her for her own ends, it sure felt that way.

She hadn't expected CJ to be like Sharon, her college ex. Sharon had wanted her expertise, too, and once she'd gotten what she needed from Leslie, she took off. She had asked Leslie to go with her but the invitation hadn't been sincere. When Leslie went to Spain to meet her, Sharon already had a new girlfriend. *Expertise.* That's what she was good for, what she could provide to further CJ's goals.

Well I'll give her my expertise. I don't need to give her my soul. I'll play the game, and when the game is played out, I'll still have myself. Maybe Boston is the best choice, after all.

Leslie finished cleaning up, dressed in her comfortable sweats and finger-combed her hair. She had forgotten her hairbrush in haste to leave the main camper area. She swiped a towel over the steam-covered mirror and looked searchingly into her own eyes. Yes, she had felt something these last few days with CJ. *Do I really want to play it safe? I don't know. Dare greatly. Stupid, for sure.*

She took a deep breath and let it out, picked up her dirty clothes and reentered the main cabin. When CJ looked up and smiled at her, she couldn't help but smile back. She tucked her clothes in the back section of her duffel and returned to the plate of steaming enchiladas. The smell was already making her mouth water.

"Thanks," she said with an appreciative sniff. "I'm starved."

CJ set a bag of chips and bowls of salsa and guacamole in front of her. Sitting down across from her and picking up her fork, she said, "Dig in. I'm hungry, too. Lunch was a sandwich on the road. It wasn't a very good sandwich either."

There was silence punctuated by sounds of appreciation as they gave the food the attention it deserved.

Finally, Leslie used a chip to coax the last bit of guacamole out of the bowl and popped it into her mouth. "That was great." She was feeling a lot more inclined to give CJ more leeway now that she had eaten.

CJ gazed at her across the table. "Better?"

Leslie sighed and patted her stomach. "Better."

"I can find someone else to work with, but I'd rather work with you. Yes, this furthers my goal and you can look at it like I'm using you. I'm not. But if you believe that, I can find someone else."

Leslie could see the earnestness in CJ's eyes.

"We have something," CJ continued, "and I don't want to contaminate that. But I need this." She made a sweeping gesture at the pile of photos and folders on the side of the table. "I need to do this. I want your help."

"I'll help you," Leslie said quietly.

CJ covered Leslie's hand, lacing their fingers and giving a light squeeze that was returned. Then Leslie took her hand back and said, "Enough schmaltz. Exactly what do you need from me?"

CJ pushed their dishes aside, pulled the folders and photos closer and explained what was needed. They talked over the various locations and climbs and the pros and cons of each— access paths, camera angles, even issues with the catering setup.

It was getting late when Leslie yawned. One more question. "Have you got permission from the Park Service for all of this?"

CJ nodded. "I assume Jerry or one his assistants has worked that out. The actual location still has to be scrubbed by the Park Service but I'm hoping you can help me with the right words and promises for the contract."

"Enough." Leslie stood. "Come to bed." She tugged CJ out of the booth. "I want more of that expertise you showed me last night."

CHAPTER FOURTEEN

The next morning, they woke to banging on the camper door.

"You expecting someone?" Leslie mumbled into the back of CJ's neck.

CJ started to mumble something back but then she leaped out of bed and reached for Leslie's discarded sweats. She pulled them on, then stumbled for the door. "It's Bonnie and Sam. They work for Jerry," she whispered to Leslie before wrenching it open.

"Hey, Sam, hey, Bonnie." Her voice was too bright. "You got here earlier than I expected. Have you guys eaten yet?"

"On the way up," Bonnie said as she looked around the campsite. "We've got rooms in town for tonight but we didn't stop. Sam wanted to see the morning lights. If you're good with it, we'll just go walk around the area and check it out."

Sam nodded.

"Sure," CJ said. "Sure. The sun will be coming up shortly. Make sure you register the car. Registration is near where you drove into the Hidden Valley campground."

Bonnie and Sam nodded their agreement and headed toward the campground entrance.

"It's six o'clock," Leslie said as she came out of the bathroom. She didn't look happy to have early-morning company.

CJ rolled her eyes. "I know. I was expecting them early but not *this* early. They must have left LA at three to get here now. But Sam is all about lighting." She pulled Leslie into a morning kiss.

"Toothbrush," Leslie muttered after returning the kiss. She turned CJ toward the bathroom and patted her ass.

A few minutes later, Leslie found Sam and Bonnie wandering back from the registration kiosk.

"I'm Leslie. I'm the climbing guide coach, helping CJ out. Is there anything specific you'd like to see?"

Bonnie said, "Sam needs to see all aspects of the light. I'm responsible for camera setups and how to make the best use of what Sam sees. We like to use as much natural light as possible… but this place looks like there's lots of shadows."

"Yes and no," Leslie said. "Midday there aren't many shadows and it can get plenty bright. We can work on that. CJ was showing me some of the locations that were put forward as possible candidates. The climbing shots should be mostly in the open, which will give you the chance for maximum light unless you want any evening or night shots."

They walked back to camp, and Leslie and CJ gathered together the climbing gear for the day. After filling everyone's travel mugs with coffee, they packed the gear and additional water in the back of the Subaru Outback the studio had provided and headed to the northern section of Wonderland.

Bonnie drove slowly, pointing and keeping up a continuous chatter about the Joshua trees and the various rock formations as the sun came up. Sam remained quiet but his head was on a constant swivel as he tried to take everything in as they drove back toward the park's west entrance. When they got to the Key's Corner parking area, Leslie pointed to where they needed to go next. Bonnie followed her instructions and drove as far in as was allowed.

"We'll have to walk in from here," Leslie said once Bonnie had parked.

Bonnie jumped out of the car. She was staring in wonder at the various rock formations, where the sun was coming up in earnest over the walls of sculpted rock.

"This granite is amazing! The texture and color pop!" Bonnie exclaimed as she touched the nearest rock wall.

Leslie stood beside her. "Most people assume the rock in Joshua Tree National Park is granite, but it's actually monzogranite. That's still granite, but there's a difference. Granite is a very hard, granular, crystalline igneous rock that consists mainly of quartz, mica, and feldspar. Monzogranite is also a type of igneous rock but it belongs to a biotite type of granite that is considered to be the final fractionation product of magma. It's a hard, fine-grained type of metasomatite, or essentially altered basalt. It's more resistant to acids and less resistant to wind."

Bonnie stared at her. "You seem to know a lot about this."

Leslie shrugged. "I love the climbing and the way Joshua Tree makes me feel but I also like the science of it."

"Any more fun facts?"

"Just one more." She smiled. "For fun. The monzogranite developed in a system of joints oriented horizontally formed by the erosion of water and flash floods, vertically paralleling surrounding rocks, and a second vertical occurring at high angles, creating the huge rectangular blocks we see. It almost doesn't look real in some places." She waved toward the formation in front of them. "I like the surreal look. Like a child god's playground."

Bonnie and Sam laughed.

Leslie turned to find CJ staring at her. "What?"

"I guess I'll have to add nerdy geologist to my list for you." Before Leslie could respond, CJ said, "Well, we better get moving if we want to catch the light Sam wants."

They pulled gear out of the car. Sam and Bonnie grabbed camera equipment and tripods while Leslie and CJ handled the climbing gear. When everybody had water and they were all loaded up, Leslie took point and started up the Wonderland

Trail toward The Ivory Tower and Timbuktu Towers. It was a fair hike in and they went slowly as Bonnie and Sam studied the area and took photos and video.

CJ peppered Leslie with questions about the location: the best paths to bring equipment into the area, staging areas for the massive amount of gear any film crew required. Leslie answered her questions as best she could while watching to make sure Bonnie and Sam didn't stray too far from the route they were taking. There were lots of interesting climbing spots in this area and it was easy to get lost if you didn't know where you were going.

Finally arriving at the Towers, Leslie pointed to the approaches and angles she thought would work best. Bonnie and Sam again took photos and video from various angles. Sam also pulled out a notebook and made sketches, noting the angles of the sun and the times.

As Leslie and CJ set up for Leslie to climb Chain of Addiction on The Ivory Tower, Bonnie and Sam set up several cameras to shoot the climb. Once they were satisfied that they had the angles they wanted, they waved for Leslie to begin climbing.

It was good, Leslie thought, that they had taken so long to set up the various shots, as it gave her time to study the climb. It was a new climb for her and had some tricky spots and a good challenge. She was eager to get on the rock. Climbing was easier than thinking about the future.

She wished Joe or Tom were here to help with the Beta on this one but she knew she was going to have to figure it out on her own. Although she had visualized each handhold and foot placement for the first twenty feet, she had to guess above that. Vogel's guidebook said it had nine bolts and was at the center of The Ivory Tower's north face. Nothing else.

She checked her helmet strap and harness once more. She had quickdraws this time, which were lengths of strong webbing with carabiners at each end. One carabiner was for the bolts on the face of the climb, the second, for her to clip the rope into as she climbed. She checked that she had enough of them, then took a deep breath. She was ready.

She nodded to CJ, who nodded back at her, then she climbed onto the rock. She made her way slowly, meticulously, from minor granite flake to slight depression, managing her handholds and foot placements carefully and with no wasted motion or energy. She clipped in as she went, making her way steadily up the rock. At one point a foot slipped and it looked like she was going to fall but she steadied herself and downclimbed a step to reset her feet, pulled through the overhang and ascended to the top. She was breathing heavily when she finished. She couldn't believe she had made it with only the one small fumble. No falls.

Bonnie and Sam applauded.

Leslie smiled down at them and waved. "This what you're looking for?" she called.

They both gave her a thumbs-up. She stayed on top of the rock enjoying the spectacular view as Sam and Bonnie rechecked lighting measurements and fussed with camera angles. When they were done, CJ lowered her down to repeat a couple of small segments of the climb. Afterward, when Leslie regained the top, she found a rappel bolt. After letting CJ know she was going off rope, she reset the rope for a rappel down the face so she could retrieve the quickdraws.

"This is awesome!" Bonnie gushed as they sat down to eat lunch. "So cool! I think we got what we need for this climb. Do you think we can do Astro Dome today, too?"

Leslie checked her watch. "It's a haul, but we can look at the area. We may be walking out in the dark, though. Astro Dome is part of Wonderland but it's on the south side. It's probably easier to go back to the car and drive to the Wonderland parking area. There's more to it—big wall climbing, multi-pitch, meaning more than one rope will be required to do the climb. I'd rather have a third person if we do this climb." She knew that CJ could not do the climb. If they were going to do a multi-pitch, she'd need an experienced climber. While she wasn't willing to rat CJ out as inexperienced, she didn't want to promise something she couldn't deliver.

They finished up at the Chain of Addiction and headed back to the car. The hike back was much quicker than the hike in, as this time they didn't slow down for photos or conversation. It was a nice silence. Leslie had always enjoyed quiet moments on the trails through the multiple rock formations. The light and the gentle breeze added to the magical landscape. At one point CJ had slipped her hand into Leslie's and pulled her off the path for a quick kiss before they caught up with the others.

After they arrived at the Wonderland parking area, Leslie again took the lead, taking them past the Indian Wave boulders and heading toward Astro Dome. Bonnie and Sam took more photos and video and Bonnie kept up a running commentary. Because they had all gotten into a rhythm, it didn't take them as long to get to the Astro Dome formation. At the area, Leslie watched CJ sketch out placements for equipment and personnel.

"The trailers will have to stay on the roadways. I don't think they will be able to drive into these locations. And catering will have to be limited to what can be carried in for the day."

"I agree. The area is fragile and I'm sure it wouldn't be approved by the park service. You'll have to get permits for any drone footage you want."

"Right, I'll add that to my list. What do you think about building walkways to ensure the integrity of the site?"

Leslie nodded approvingly. CJ had been listening when she mentioned limiting foot traffic and the problems with getting lost in the area.

As Bonnie and Sam set up cameras for the Astro Dome climb, Leslie again scoped out the climb. She'd be doing only part of it. They had agreed to come back the next day if she could find a willing third climber. Knowing that, Leslie was okay with leaving a couple of quickdraws in place overnight. She knew several climbers who had put together awesome racks of equipment, cleaning climbs where others had left gear in place on the routes. There were lots of reasons people left gear. Sudden storms. Lack of time. More money than sense.

Once Bonnie and Sam were ready with cameras, Leslie did her self-check and then checked CJ. Ready to go. Leslie climbed to the top of the first pitch on The Gunslinger.

It wasn't easy and she was still tired from climbing Chain of Addiction. She fell twice. The second fall happened when she was clipping in and missed the clip. She fell almost twenty feet. CJ had called out to her, asking if she was okay, but she was tired and ragged when she finally let CJ belay her down, removing all of the low quickdraws as she came.

And so it was a tired bunch that headed back to the car. Their headlamps illuminated the shadowy path. At Indian Wave Boulders, Sam stopped, turned off his headlamp and just looked up at the night sky. It was getting dark rapidly and the stars were starting to become visible.

"Sam's an amateur astronomer," Bonnie explained. "Come on, Sam. We'll stop on the way back to the hotel and you can look all you want."

Leslie laughed. "It's a beautiful place, isn't it?"

Bonnie turned to her with a smile. "I think Jerry is going to be very happy."

Bonnie and Sam dropped CJ and Leslie back at the campsite before heading to their hotel in Yucca Valley. They'd be back at five the next morning, as Sam wanted to see the sunrise again and judge lighting hues. He also wanted to set up and film the location during the morning hours, so they were going to stop at the Key's Corner parking area again. They said they wouldn't pick up CJ and Leslie until nine.

CJ exchanged a few words with Bonnie before turning to Leslie, who was schlepping the gear back into the camper. What a fabulous day, she thought. It had been beyond her expectations that she would have so much information to use to put her plan together. Leslie had been amazing. Yes, this was going to work. Another couple of days and she'd have what she needed to wow Brad, and Brad to wow Jerry. Picking up the last of the gear, she followed Leslie into the camper.

"Have you figured out who you're going have help you on the multi-pitch?" CJ asked, looking in the fridge to see what they could make for dinner. "I know I can't climb that, though I do appreciate you not saying that in front of Bonnie and Sam."

"Sam is interesting." Leslie was sorting through the gear she had laid out on the bed. "I think he said two sentences all day." Mimicking Sam's voice, she said, "Wow. Awesome."

CJ grinned and pulled leftover spaghetti sauce out of the fridge. "Why should he talk when he has Bonnie to talk for him? She wasn't talking as much as she normally does, though. I think the only time she is truly quiet is when the camera is actually rolling for production."

Setting the warmed-up sauce on the dinette, she turned to Leslie and pulled her close and whispered, "You are magnificent. I saw the rating on that climb. I agree with Sam. Wow, just wow." She nuzzled Leslie's neck and then leaned back before leaning in again to kiss her softly on the lips.

The kiss heated them up, clothes came off and landed haphazardly on the floor. Leslie's sudden harsh intake of breath as CJ tugged at Leslie's climbing pants made her stop. As the waistline of the pants came down, she could see some bruising starting to form.

"Ouch!" CJ said. "From the fall?"

"Comes with the territory," Leslie said, stepping out of the pants. "You'd be surprised at how many strange cuts and bruises I get that I don't know about until I take my shower."

She pulled CJ closer and they quickly shed their remaining clothing. Slowly and with great care, they continued their explorations of each other. Soon they fell onto the bed, their bodies entwined.

Later, CJ rested her head on Leslie's shoulder as they snuggled. "I'm hungry," she announced.

"That's the one problem with JT," Leslie replied, stroking CJ's shoulder with a fingertip. "No delivery. Although I heard they're thinking about it. I expect if you paid enough, though, you could get anything delivered." She stopped for another kiss. "So this is your world," Leslie mused. "It was a fun day but I'm not sure I could handle waiting for the camera angles and the light to be just right every day."

CJ cuddled closer. "The days are different. Some days are like this, some days, there's a lot of sitting around and waiting."

"Well, we're not getting any less hungry, are we? I'll make spaghetti and you review what you've got so far. We can work more on this later."

"Put some clothes on or I won't be able to concentrate," CJ said with a hint of mischief as she languidly stretched before retrieving her bag.

Leslie laughed and complied.

They sat next to each other at the dinette for dinner. Leslie had toasted some bread and spread garlic on it, which they wolfed down while waiting for the spaghetti to cook. Beer wasn't the perfect accompaniment but it would serve in camp.

As they were polishing off a bag of cookies Leslie had found, CJ said, "I think I have the basics of what I need for the plan. Who are you going to get to climb Astro Dome with you?"

"I'd like it to be Tom or Joe but they can't get here tomorrow." Leslie reached for her phone. "But let me text Adam. He's the guy I was climbing with on Thursday when you went back to LA Maybe he or one of his group would be willing to do a multi-pitch, even though I think they specialize in bouldering."

Adam responded and Leslie went off to talk to him at a nearby campsite, leaving CJ alone with her thoughts and the dishes. Brad was expecting her to be climbing. She had the same build as the female lead. And with movie magic, she could probably double for Brendon Lewis, the male lead, too. But she couldn't climb like Leslie. Seeing Leslie fall had scared her badly and seeing the bruises had reinforced how dangerous climbing could be. Especially the second fall. Leslie had just hung there for several excruciating seconds before her calls had been answered. Mistakes could be fatal. For most stunts, the greatest fear was injury. That wasn't always true, of course, but there had been enough shoots that were stopped when a stunt person was killed during filming. Great care was taken that that didn't happen, but sometimes it did.

CJ knew that her plan would need to be clear, concise, and ultimately safe, with Leslie doing the climbing. If Adam panned out for the multi-pitch, she'd have to sell that to Brad and potentially Jerry as well. She wanted a rep—a good rep—as a stunt coordinator. This was her chance to skip the stunts and go straight to coordinator. Yes, it could work if she put together the right team. Bonnie and Sam were good and she could count on them to get the right perspectives. She didn't need to worry about aspects of lighting, as Sam had that down. She would, however, need to work with the location people. There would need to be a lot of coordination with the Park Service concerning the sites they had picked to ensure that the fragile environment would be protected.

She had noted the Access Fund trail headers that encouraged climbers and hikers to stay on the maintained trails. The environmental conditions and the lack of rain could make going off trail damage the environment for years. The good news/bad news scenario was that the film industry could bring a lot of money and good publicity to the park...as well as more foot traffic that might damage fragile ecosystems.

CJ turned as the camper door opened and Leslie came in, turning off her headlamp. "So?" CJ inquired. "What did he say?"

Leslie shrugged out of her jacket. "It's getting colder out there. Adam says he doesn't have the right skills to do the routes."

CJ moaned.

"However, Jacob does, and he's good. I didn't know he was in camp, but Adam pulled him over after he got my text."

"Jacob?"

"You picked the right time to come to JT. Wintertime is the season world-class climbers come here to hone their skills. It seems that there is just such a group of climbers from Spain in camp this week. Jacob Medina is one of them. I hadn't met him before but I know him by reputation. He's done some big wall climbing in Spain and Italy. He's good. Better yet, he's willing to help."

"Does he know we'll be filming him?"

"Yes, he's good with that. He wants to get a line in the credits. He says it will thrill his mother." Leslie smiled. "The Spanish and their moms."

"I think I can work that out," CJ said, making a note. "The real filming isn't going to be for several months, probably early February. Will he be available to come back?"

"Most likely. The guys seemed excited about the prospect. If you pay their expenses, they'll be happy. There are three of them but Jacob's really what you're looking for." Leslie came across the room to sit next to CJ. "I might not be here in February, though."

CJ could feel her pulse quicken. With all the activity, she had forgotten about Leslie's trip to Boston. "Do you have to go? I know you're a programmer but you could work on this film with me."

"I made a commitment," Leslie said, no enthusiasm in her voice.

"A commitment to go to Boston to see what they have to offer," CJ said. "You didn't promise to move. Not yet." Her words seemed to be more of a plea than a statement.

"I hear you, CJ, but AZM's offer is really good and all you can offer me is a few months of work. I need a secure job. I really want to help you but I need to think about my future too."

"How long will you be in Boston?"

"Four days. I come back on Friday."

Neither wanted to push on the topic further.

The next two days were much like Wednesday, with Bonnie and Sam arriving early and the team scouting the climbs. Jacob and his friends, Luis and Freddie, now rounded out the group. Their teasing banter and flirting manner with Bonnie were fun to watch. Leslie joined in the banter but left the flirting to the others. CJ listened as she worked the climb with Jacob on the multi-pitch approach. CJ found it fascinating how the discussions built up a mutual trust and confidence in each other's climbing abilities and quirks. Luis and Freddie helped with the Beta on the climb, but when Leslie and Jacob started up The Gunslinger, they left to go climb on some nearby formations.

CJ stepped back and used the time to create the plan. She also watched, spellbound, as Leslie and Jacob progressed up the route. She used binoculars and camera views to see how they set up the anchors at each transition point. Sam had put up a drone camera, though he kept it low, never going above the formation. The climb looked intricate from the ground, almost as if Leslie and Jacob were climbing a blank wall of solid rock. Only with the visual support could CJ see the flakes and slight outcroppings or slopes in the rock face.

She used her notes from the climb and supplemented them with footage to detail each stage and step of the climbs. It took them more than six hours to run the four pitches. When Leslie rejoined her on the ground, she said six hours was actually very fast, considering the amount of anchoring and cleaning they'd had to do. CJ knew that the actual amount of footage in the film would be on the order of minutes, not hours.

It was her job to provide the plan that would support the narrative Jerry wanted. She stayed up late each night, reviewing the footage Sam and Bonnie had collected and her notes and diagrams from the day. The plan was coming together but it would be touch-and-go if she could complete it for the Monday morning session.

Leslie supported her but didn't push as CJ's tension increased. CJ didn't go to bed at night until she was practically collapsing from exhaustion. Leslie, tired from climbing all day, went to bed only to wake in the middle of night to CJ's typing and paper rustling. In the morning, CJ extricated herself from the bed to make coffee and preview her notes for the new day.

It was late Sunday night when CJ reviewed what she had with the team and asked for their input and suggestions. "I meet with Brad at ten tomorrow and then Brad has a meeting with Jerry at one in the afternoon," she explained with as much energy as she could manage. "I want to thank you for all the effort you've put into the last couple of days to make this come together. Jacob, thanks for all your help and willingness to jump into this project. The casting director will call you and provide you with the timelines for when we'll need you again. I may be calling with questions, though." She paused. "Bonnie, Sam, it's always a pleasure working with you. I think you got what you needed as well?"

Bonnie and Sam nodded.

"I'll see you back on the lot Monday, then."

After they had left, CJ slumped on the picnic bench at the campsite. Leslie had put up solar lighting to brighten the area and it gave off a soft glow. CJ felt tired but satisfied. After a minute, she got up and put her arms around Leslie, hugging her tight.

"The plan is about as good as I can make it," she murmured into Leslie's ear. "And working any more on it is just nitpicking. I couldn't have done this without you. You've been a rock. My rock." Laughing a little, she kissed Leslie softly.

She knew she was leaving early the next morning to get back to LA and beat the morning traffic. They hadn't talked about the future. Boston was hanging solidly between them.

This was their last night together in Joshua Tree. CJ didn't want to bring up topics like Boston or the future. Even though her concentration had been on the stunt planning, she knew Leslie had been worrying about her upcoming trip. She was worried about Leslie's trip to Boston, too, but she didn't want to overstep. She wanted Leslie to stay and for them to discover what they could be together outside the cloistered environment of Joshua Tree National Park.

"Come to bed," CJ said, pulling Leslie toward the camper. "Let's make the most of the night."

CHAPTER FIFTEEN

After Leslie had kissed CJ goodbye at five a.m., she'd had a hard time going back to sleep, though she finally managed to drift off. The sun was coming in through the slats when she woke up at seven twenty-five. She groaned and got slowly out of bed. She had promised Jacob another day of climbing. His friends had left on Saturday and he'd stayed to help with the filming and production planning. They had agreed to meet this morning and go try out a climb on Jerry's Quarry on the Geology Tour Road. Located southeast of Hidden Valley, Jerry's Quarry was a complex set of boulders and rocks with some classic traditional climbs that she hadn't done in a while. She thought Jacob would enjoy them.

She needed to get back to Los Angeles to pack and pick up her tickets before her flight tomorrow. But she wasn't in any hurry. Her only time constraint was getting the RV to the Black Rock dump site and then dropping it back at Zero G. The flight was early in the morning and she could sleep on the plane.

So her plan for today was to climb and try to regain both balance and perspective. Jacob had become a friend. They had put their lives in each other's hands over the last couple of days and had built a rapport. Jacob knew that she and CJ were together but that it was new and fragile.

She was finishing breakfast when he knocked on the door and came into the camper, his tall, lean frame filling the doorway. He pushed a lock of blue-black hair back from his forehead, his white teeth flashing against his tan face.

"Are you ready?" he asked in his smooth, slightly accented English. "The temperature is starting to rise and the chill is leaving the air."

Leslie finished her last swallow of coffee and put her cup in the sink. Grabbing her gear, she followed him to his rental car, which was full of rock-climbing paraphernalia and food wrappers. She threw the detritus in the backseat and climbed in. "Do you know the way?" she asked, her mind filling in the music and lyrics, "to San Jose?" though she didn't say the last part out loud.

Jacob smiled as he took his place in the driver's seat. "Sí. I have been there a couple of times with my friends. There is good climbing and not too many people. Most climbers do not want to go out there, as it is far from the camp."

The road to Jerry's Quarry was south down Park Boulevard, then east down Geology Tour Road, which turned into a bumpy, sandy unpaved road.

"You sure about driving this car here?" she asked.

He jerked the steering wheel to miss a hole. "No problem. We are not going that far. We will stop at pullout number five."

They found the pullout and Jacob parked the car. Then they headed down the trail to the formation.

"The beautiful CJ has gone back to LA," said Jacob, dropping his gear and turning to look at her. "You did not go with her."

Leslie sighed. "No."

He pulled on his harness and sat on a rock to put on his shoes. "Why do you let her get away from you?"

She fastened her harness and sat down to put on her shoes. "It's complicated," she said as she tied her shoelaces and pulled the rope from the bag.

"Beautiful women are always complicated," he said. "Two women more so."

She laughed but it almost came out as a sob. "Oh, I don't know if men aren't just as complicated."

He simply smiled at her.

"I've got a potential job in another city. It's a bad time to start up a new relationship."

He nodded sympathetically but did not comment.

"I don't know if she wants me or my expertise. Maybe I'm just a convenience."

His eyebrows rose high enough to be lost under the wave of his hair. Then he laughed. "You are missing the point of love. Love is many things. You do not love someone for just one piece of themselves. Is climbing not a part of you?"

"But does she only want me to further her goals?"

"It did not appear that way to me." He shrugged his shoulders. "But I am not familiar with your ways. You did not see her watching you when you climbed or when you fell."

"I've made a commitment to go to Boston. I need the work. And the structure."

He looked at her for a long moment. "You need to go to keep your word, but is it really structure you want? Or are you running away from that balance you seek?"

They spent the day climbing and enjoying the simple comaraderie that came with working through complex problems with both body and mind. The day was warm and they rested often, talking about climbing and their respective jobs.

"Do you like designing websites?" he asked as they sat in the shade after completing another difficult route.

"I find it similar to climbing," she said after she'd taken a sip from her water bottle. "It's a problem to be solved creatively with a beginning, a middle, and an end." She took another sip. "How about you? Do you enjoy working for your father in his textile business?"

"He gives me a lot of freedom to travel. As long as I am home for holidays to see my mother, I do not do anything to embarrass the family, and I spend at least some of my time talking with our clients, it is all good."

It was past two when they started back to camp. He needed to get back to Los Angeles to talk to his father's clients and she needed to get to the RV dump site before heading back to the city herself.

"Have you climbed in the Gunks?" Leslie asked, using the climbers' slang for the Shawangunks near New Paltz, New York.

"Once," he said. "It was summertime and the bugs were bigger than the rocks." Seeing the look on her face, he added, "I think it was just the wrong time of the year."

"If I move to Boston, outdoor climbing may be hard to come by," she said, "though there do seem to be some locations within a few hours' drive, like the Quincy Quarries. But they all seem small in comparison to the variety here. The Gunks is the closest I can find to JT and its wide variety of climbing."

After Jacob pulled into his campsite at Hidden Valley and they parted company with a quick hug, Leslie walked back to Tom's camper and began readying her own departure. She knew she was on an emotional roller coaster and her stomach felt like it was between drops.

CHAPTER SIXTEEN

"You aren't in these pictures," Brad said as he perused the photos of Ivory Tower and Astro Dome. "Great shots, to be sure, but these aren't you." He turned to face CJ. "Did you sell me a bill of goods?"

"I can climb," she replied. "Just not at the level I think you and Jerry are looking for. But I got you some great climbers and a complete plan. You and Jerry can decide which pieces or parts you want to use. How you want to stage things. I'll make sure the situation is safe for the stunt people and the actors. I think you'd rather have me give you a workable plan than one that could get someone killed."

Brad looked surprised by her vehemence.

"Doing it wrong can get you killed," CJ repeated emphatically.

He grunted in acknowledgment and returned to studying the step-by-step breakdown, thumbing through the sketches, pictures, diagrams, and equipment lists. It was several pages long. When he finally finished reading, he sat back. "You've really thought this through. Bonnie and Sam said Leslie and Jacob were amazing."

It was CJ's turn to look surprised but then she frowned. Of course, Bonnie would report in, though she'd be surprised if Sam had said anything.

"Sam said he was impressed, too," Brad said, noting her look of astonishment. "He does talk occasionally, you know, and Bonnie can be quiet. I did keep tabs on you in Joshua Tree. I think it's good enough for a first go with Jerry at one o'clock. Go eat. I'll meet you back in Conference Room Five at one." He picked up another of the glossy photos in front of him, then turned to the video clips on his laptop. "I'll keep these."

As she got up to leave, he stopped her. "Good work, CJ."

She nodded her thanks and headed back to her truck. She had done the truly hard. Next up—the impossible. Jerry.

She called Leslie and when she didn't answer, she texted her. No response. She had two hours before the next meeting. She texted Sally and they agreed to meet for lunch.

Sally was already seated at a window table when CJ arrived. She put down her phone when CJ sat down across from her.

"You did it," Sally gushed. "You created the climbing plan for *On the Edge*. That was quick work! Well done! Sad to hear about Jack's fall but I hear he wouldn't listen to that coach's advice, Joe or something. Jack isn't usually so reckless and Jill is usually a calming influence when he is. Their loss was your gain."

CJ smiled. "I never wished them ill, but Jack gave Leslie a bad time too. Not sure what's up with that, though climbing is much harder than it looks, especially when you get to the harder climbs. And if you have any fear of heights, well…it can be scary."

"Maybe that was it. Anyway, look at you. When is your meeting with Jerry?"

"At one o'clock."

Sally checked her watch. "That's soon. What's your plan? Are you going to present or will Brad?"

"Brad didn't say," CJ said, looking at the menu.

Sally accepted a menu from the waiter and waited until he had explained the day's specials and walked away before she continued. "Jerry's a funny guy. Intense one minute, joking with everyone the next. If you do present, be ready for anything. Be relaxed but don't be too relaxed."

CJ waved her hands. "Enough! I'm already nervous and you're not helping at all. I've got this."

"I know you do." Sally sounded contrite. "You've dealt with people in the film industry all your life. I'm just really excited for you and I want...well, I want it to go well."

"I know you do." She paused. "I do need your help with something both personal and professional."

Sally waited.

CJ sighed. "I don't know quite how to say this. Leslie is my lead climber for the stunts. She may be moving out of state. And I might be falling for her."

"Wait—what? Slow down and start over."

"Leslie is the climbing coach from Zero G. She was supposed to be the one training Jack and Jill. Jack ticked her off somehow. I convinced her to help me and we went out to Joshua Tree National Park."

"Camping?" Sally looked shocked.

While they ate, CJ filled her in on the adventures of the last few days with Leslie and the crew at Joshua Tree.

"Let me get this straight. You have qualified experts," Sally said through a mouthful of sandwich. "So what's the problem?"

"Well, professionally, I billed myself as the expert climber." CJ was pushing her salad around on the plate. "That's how I got the job. Brad accepts my excuse on that one, but it doesn't add any gloss to my rep."

"Okay. So, what about Leslie?"

"I think Leslie thinks I'm just using her. She's going to Boston tomorrow for a job interview."

Sally waited.

"I don't want her to take that job. Professionally, I need her."

"And personally?"

"And personally, I want to be with her," CJ said quietly. "I just don't know how to blend the personal with the professional. Am I just enamored with her because of my professional goals or am I really falling for her? I just know I don't want her to leave."

"Have you told her how you feel?"

CJ looked up at her friend. "This is *me* we're talking about. When have I ever told someone how I feel?"

"Well," Sally said, "your roommate in college, but we know where that got you. Okay. Well, first, you have to get through Jerry. Then you need to figure out what's next for you and Leslie."

"But if I don't have Leslie, how do I sell what I have to Jerry?"

"Can you replace Leslie if you have to?"

"I don't know. I don't want to."

"Want and reality are two different things."

CJ rubbed her face again. "Maybe. But she's good, really good. I'd have to get a professional climber to replace her."

"She's that good?"

"She's that good."

"And she's leaving tomorrow." Sally dragged a fry through the ketchup on her plate and ate it slowly. "When does she get back? Do you expect her to come back?"

"Friday. She gets back on Friday."

"And when are you seeing her again? Tonight?"

"We didn't make plans. I just left this morning."

Sally covered her eyes with her hand.

"I know, I know. I should have said something sweet, endearing, loving, professed my undying love. But I didn't know what to say."

Sally dropped her hand. "Well, girl, you need to do something. She's leaving for Boston tomorrow. She doesn't know how you feel and she must want this job if she's willing to travel across the country for a job interview."

"They want her. They've already offered her the job. She's just going to see if she wants to accept."

"All the more reason you need to do something. Something dramatic. With feeling." Sally was waving her arms like she was creating a vision.

"She's a quiet person, not given to big demonstrations. I don't think dramatic is what she'd want."

"*Everybody* likes dramatic. You can do quiet dramatic. Hmm, let me think. Flowers. Chocolate. You need to do something to make her want to come back to you. Is she here in LA or still camping?" Sally sniffed disdainfully as she said the word "camping."

"She's driving the RV back to Zero G tonight. She'll fly out of LAX tomorrow morning."

"Well, then you need to be at Zero G when she gets there with something to show your appreciation of her and her charms. Before she leaves and travels across the US, she needs to want to come back to you."

CJ gave this some thought. "Well, first, I need to get through Jerry and this meeting. What can I promise and what do I hedge?"

"Promise outstanding climbing for his film. You don't need to mention Leslie not being the one doing the climbing. Not yet, anyway."

The waiter brought the bill. CJ paid it and waited until he had cleared the table. "I don't want to mislead Brad again."

"Tough situation. Will Leslie come back for you? For the filming, if she takes the job?"

"I don't know."

"Ask her! Now go be brilliant and tell Sally everything when it's over. This is so exciting. I love living vicariously." She gave CJ a hug in the parking lot, murmuring, "You've got this."

CJ nodded and drove back to the studio, her mind more on Leslie than the upcoming meeting around which her life goals depended.

At nine fifteen that evening, Leslie pulled into the Zero G parking area. The drive from Joshua Tree had been more brutal than normal. An accident on the I-10 had jammed up traffic for miles and now she was tired and hungry. Grabbing her gear, she headed toward her car to drop everything before going into Zero G to give Tom the keys.

She didn't see the big pink cardboard heart until she opened the passenger door. It was wedged under the driver's side wiper blade. She carefully closed the passenger door and walked to the other side to pull it off.

Bold letters across the front spelled out *MISS YOU. COME BACK TO ME. CJ*. Opening the driver's door, Leslie sat heavily in the seat. She'd been wondering about CJ all day. How was the meeting going? Was she okay? Was she thinking about me at all? Well, here was part of the answer. Yes, CJ was thinking about her. Leslie felt an ache go through her. It wasn't February, so CJ had had to take the time to make this faux Valentine. Leslie felt tears in the corners of her eyes. She ran a quick sleeve across her eyes and carefully stowed the heart on top of her gear.

When she entered the gym, a few climbers cheered her. She was surprised, as climbers were usually pretty laid back, so why were they cheering her? Then she saw CJ talking to Tom, who was standing behind the counter. She waved at her climbing friends and headed over to the counter, where CJ hesitated, then reached out to hug her. Leslie walked into her embrace.

"CJ was telling me about the meeting with Jerry," said Tom, who sounded pleased. "They like what you guys put together this past week."

Leslie let go of CJ and stepped back. "I'm glad. It was fun."

Tom's eyes were twinkling. "It looks like it."

She passed him the keys. "Thanks for the loan of the RV. This one is much nicer than the previous one. I didn't get a chance to run it through the carwash."

He waved her off. "No worries, I'll have Joe do it tomorrow."

Leslie turned to CJ. "So how did the meeting go? You good?"

"There's a couple of minor things but basically they loved what they saw." CJ smiled at her. "They may even use some of what Bonnie and Sam shot this weekend. I was a little excited when I came in here to tell you. You weren't here, though, so I told Tom. He shared and got some of your friends excited." She waved at the climbers in the gym. "Brad and Jerry loved your climbing and the sites we picked," she added. "And they liked Jacob and he'll work in fine. But they really loved you." There was a glow in CJ's eyes as she looked at Leslie.

Leslie wasn't sure if the glow was for her or for her work. Before she could think about it too much, however, CJ touched her arm. "You hungry? I only ate some snacks at the meeting and it ran long. I was hoping you'd join me for dinner."

As if on cue, Tom backed away and headed for his office. "I'll let you two chat," he said over his shoulder. He gave Leslie a thumbs-up that only she saw.

Was everyone a matchmaker?

"I need to get home and pack," Leslie said, suddenly feeling grumpy. It had been a long day and driving in bumper-to-bumper traffic is never fun.

CJ nodded. "Then will I see you when you get back?"

Seeing the look in CJ's eyes, Leslie relented at little. "I'll call you from Boston tomorrow and you can tell me all about the meeting."

CJ smiled. "Great, I'll talk to you then." She turned for the door. "Have a safe trip," she said, and then she was gone.

Tom came back out of the office. "You should have gone with her. You're hungry."

"I know, and I'm confused. CJ confuses me and I hate being confused. And yes, I'm starving." She grabbed a Kind Bar from the rack, ripped it open and ate it in four bites.

"She likes you…that's obvious."

"I wasn't ready to say goodbye again tomorrow." She grabbed a Stinger Honey Waffle snack next.

"Great dinner." Tom pulled the Stinger out of her hand. He reached behind the counter, grabbed an apple from a bag and handed it to her.

Leslie chomped down greedily.

"Camper came in handy," he said.

She stopped eating and grinned at him.

CHAPTER SEVENTEEN

Leslie was still tired and grumpy when she arrived at the hotel in Boston the next day. She hadn't slept well before she'd gone to the airport, and even though AZM had provided a first-class ticket for her, she hadn't slept on the plane either. Airline food was airline food, no matter how you traveled, though she had to admit that if you traveled, first-class was the way to go. The lines had been short and the service good.

She dropped her bag in her hotel room and noted that she had a message on the phone. It was similar to the note left at the front desk for her: Mia welcoming her to Boston and checking to see if she'd like to go out to dinner.

What she really wanted was just to crawl into bed but she'd promised herself that she would give this opportunity a serious chance. It was everything her career-minded, risk-averse self wanted. She called the number on the note and made plans to meet Mia downstairs in half an hour.

It was three in the afternoon in Los Angeles. She thought about contacting CJ. Thoughts of her were the reason for her lack of sleep. She picked up her phone and then stuffed it back into her back pocket, deciding she'd wait until after dinner to call CJ. Then she pulled the phone back out of her pocket and looked at one of the secret snaps she'd taken of CJ when she'd been working with Bonnie and Sam. Her hair was ruffled by the breeze and her eyes were focused on the rock formation Leslie had just rappelled down. She was in her element and looked confident. Leslie's heartbeat quickened. Sighing, she hit the button to close the screen and put her phone back in her pocket.

She needed to focus on Mia and this dinner.

When Leslie reached the lobby, Mia was already there. She was taller than Leslie and had fine, striking features and thick dark red hair, pulled back in a clip at the base of her neck. Leslie felt herself staring into her green eyes. She wore a crisp white shirt, a hunter green cable-knit sweater, and tailored jeans.

Leslie had washed her face, but was still in her travel attire of jeans, T-shirt, and hoodie. She was carrying her warm North Face jacket over her arm as it was really winter in Boston.

"Good to finally meet you after all the phone conversations," Mia said, shaking Leslie's hand firmly. "I thought we could go to a little Italian place I know near the Common," Mia said as she steered them toward the door. "My car is just outside."

"You don't have the Boston accent," Leslie said as she got into the car.

"Nope. I'm a transplant myself, though I can fake the accent if I try."

"Where are you from?"

Mia pulled out of the hotel parking area. "Arizona."

"You really wanted a change."

"I really like Boston. And I have family nearby," Mia told her. "I went to Brown for college, which is only about forty miles by train. I spent a lot of weekends here."

"What do you do for fun here?"

"I like the history and the water. They also have a couple of really nice lesbian bars. P-Town is close by," Mia said, easing into a parking structure just off the Boston Common.

"You mean Provincetown, aka lesbian heaven?" Leslie asked. "And you're a lesbian?"

"Yep," said Mia. "There are several of us in the office. It's a very diverse group. I think you'll like them."

Crap. I don't want to like it here.

As they walked to the Italian restaurant, Leslie noticed the frigid breeze sweeping across the Boston Common park, which was well lit, but stark. She was freezing in spite of her warm coat. She pulled her hood over her head realizing this might be one of the key negatives. "I'm not sure why AZM is pushing so hard for me to move to Boston," she said aloud as they entered the restaurant. She reluctantly removed her coat. It was warm in the restaurant but she was still chilled from the walk across the park.

Mia took a menu from the waiter. "Clients like you." Leslie accepted her own menu and waited for the bus person to leave their water and depart.

It was true. Clients liked her. She listened a lot and spoke little. When clients saw the final website she'd designed for them, it usually had everything they wanted and more, and it was more creative than they had imagined. Occasionally there was a conflict, but her solutions worked. Rarely was the client unsatisfied. "Most of my clients are in Los Angeles," she said, "not Boston."

"We want to expand that," Mia told her. "Boston has a great need for your talent. And New York is close by."

"My style works in LA," Leslie replied, gesturing around the room and then looking pointedly down at her jeans and hoodie. "The East Coast is more formal than California and I'm not a formal person."

Mia laughed. "Sid Baker said you would try to 'unsell' yourself. But we need your creativity. We have people who can sell." She signaled to the waiter that they were ready to order, then turned back to Leslie. "Let's enjoy the meal, and I'll tell you a little about what we do at AZM and how Mediasoft fits with our business goals."

They spent a pleasant two hours eating excellent Italian food in a warm, inviting atmosphere. Mia talked about AZM's goals, objectives, and prospects for the future. She made Boston sound like fun and the work inspiring. She even mentioned that they had a working arrangement with Harvard University for continuing education. *Harvard!*

Leslie also found Mia to be very easy on the eyes. When Mia dropped her at the hotel, she walked slowly to her room. She had a lot to think about and she didn't really know where to start. She'd thought she'd have a better idea after talking to Mia. It was actually worse. Everything Mia mentioned made it seem like the only correct choice was moving to Boston.

As Mia had said, AZM wanted her creativity, though they didn't seem to understand that her creativity came from working the entire problem. It was just like climbing. You didn't just start and finish in the middle. She liked meeting with the clients, understanding what they were trying to accomplish, building the website and then collaborating with the clients to ensure that website met all of their objectives. While Mia hadn't specifically said she would be out of the loop with the client, Mia had certainly insinuated it.

Yet there were good things about AZM, too. It was inclusive and diverse. The business model and prospects were outstanding and she'd be in line for options on the company's future. The way Mia had phrased it, they were looking at an IPO in two years' time. The current backers, Angel Investors, had real money to spend, and getting Mediasoft was one of the keys to taking the company public. *And I'll be on the ground floor to make that happen.* Exciting times to be sure. But they wanted her in Boston.

Six of the seventeen Mediasoft employees had agreed to move, though names had not been provided. Sid was going to be transferred to San Francisco. Mia wouldn't talk about what he'd be doing there.

Back in Los Angeles, Leslie had done a lot of her creative work at home or outdoors. She loved sitting at a picnic table near the beach or at a campsite and working through a website's intricacies. She couldn't image sitting outside in a Boston winter.

She checked her phone as she entered her hotel room and found a text from CJ saying she would be in a planning meeting until ten o'clock or later, so their phone call would have to wait. Even though it was only eight p.m. in Los Angeles, she was exhausted from lack of sleep, a big plate of lasagna and information overload. Mia would be picking her up for the office meeting at nine in the morning.

She looked longingly at her phone again. She so wanted to talk with CJ. She texted CJ, *Call U tomorrow night*. She hesitated, then added, *Miss U.*

Yes, she thought, sitting at the table with Mia made her miss CJ's easy-going manner and great smile. Sure, Mia was stunning. That's not to say CJ wasn't beautiful, too, but she was so real. And she missed her warmth. She pulled the pink heart out of her bag and set it on the dresser.

Leslie's next few days were filled with meeting people, hearing about her future duties and checking out the local area. She had an appointment with a local realtor who showed her rental properties near the AZM office. It was all, she noticed, geared toward her accepting the offer. Someone was with her at every meal, too, which left her little time to be alone and think, and the pressure to accept the offer seemed intense. But as the pressure rose, so did her desire to push back. She didn't really understand this reluctance as AZM was hitting every point on her checklist.

The hardest part was that due to her schedule and CJ's, they never had time to do more than exchange a few quick texts. It seemed as if their work was pulling them further apart.

She needed to talk. Calling her parents wasn't helpful. They were pushing for Boston and stability. They didn't see the problems that she saw with working for AZM, only the benefits. Sid wasn't very helpful either. He listened to all of her concerns and then told her it was ultimately her decision.

On Thursday night, she politely declined the invitation to dinner. It was her last night in Boston, and she'd be flying back to Los Angeles the next day after additional meetings with the creative team at AZM. She needed time alone to regroup and find some perspective.

She found a local climbing gym.

Central Rock was busy, and the music was loud when she got there. It was a bouldering-only gym, with no sport or top-roped climbs. Solving bouldering problems worked for her, as she wanted to work alone while she worked through her thoughts and feelings. Climbing always calmed her. She checked in at the desk and paid for a day pass and a chalk bag. Pulling her shoes from her bag, she locked it in a locker and proceeded to the climbing area. The multicolored tags and surfaced walls looked familiar and friendly. These were problems she could solve. The routes didn't expect anything of her but her full attention.

She climbed in earnest until the pump in her arms and fingers tips left her shaking. She got a drink from the water fountain and sat down to watch some of the better climbers work out problems she had already solved. As the evening progressed, she warmed up to climbers and shared Beta with several of them. It was all genial and easy. Why wasn't life like climbing? She said goodbye to a couple of the climbers, got her stuff, and left the gym. It had been a satisfying evening.

As she left, her phone rang. Checking the display, she answered quickly, "CJ?"

"Hey, how are you? I finally got a break."

Leslie could hear the sounds of a meeting breaking up in the background. "I'm good," she said, sounding almost as if she were asking a question and not making a statement. Now that she had CJ on the phone, she didn't know what to say. *I miss you. I don't want to be here, I want to be with you. I'm moving to Boston.* What she finally said was, "How're things with you?"

"It's really busy here. The script is being rewritten based on some of the work you and Jacob did. They're also looking to re-create some of the outdoor scenes on the soundstage. So it's hectic and fun. I wish you were here. Everybody is super excited about how good you look on camera." CJ paused. "So, how's Boston?"

"Okay." Leslie tried to project enthusiasm she didn't feel. "The people seem friendly enough and it's a great opportunity."

"When does your plane arrive back here tomorrow? Can I pick you up?"

"I get in around five. I was planning to take Lyft back to my house. Traffic around LAX during rush hour on a Friday has to be the absolute worst."

"Don't care. Let me pick you up."

Leslie was surprised. Nobody ever wanted to be at LAX on a Friday afternoon. She tried one last time. "You know it's Friday, right? The airport will be a nightmare."

"Don't care," CJ repeated. "Text me when you get in and I'll find a way to get through the mess."

CHAPTER EIGHTEEN

Leslie's flight back from Boston was uneventful, although her plane was late landing because of an earlier delayed plane. The meetings at AZM had gone well, with the exception of the last one with the senior VP, who had wanted an answer that she didn't want to give him. He had tried sweetening the deal AZM was offering her with two additional weeks of vacation a year. She had almost capitulated. But in the end, she couldn't bring herself to say yes—yet. She needed to talk with CJ.

Now she was wondering at the change in herself. The old Leslie would have said yes and been content to go along. But something had happened in the high desert and she wanted to understand what it was. Once before she had given up on happiness for security.

On landing, she texted CJ. *Landed*

A text came back instantly. *U will be met when U get off the plane*

Leslie's eyebrows went up. How was CJ going to get through security without a ticket?

As she exited the plane with the other first-class passengers, she saw a service rep holding a sign with her name on it. She walked over and introduced herself.

"I've got orders to take you out to Gate 12," he said, taking her bag from her and waving her into the electric gate-transfer cart. He set the bag on the seat beside him and they took off down the passenger concourse.

Her phone buzzed. *did U get picked up?*

She texted back confirmation as the driver pulled up to Gate 12, where a second service rep opened a door to a jetway.

"Down this way," said the woman, who was wearing a fancy jumpsuit with a Hangar 21 logo. "Jim will be taking care of you."

The cart driver followed her down the jetway stairs to a car waiting at the bottom. He handed her bag to her, and when she called after him to give him a tip, he just waved her off with a smile. She turned to the driver. "Now what?" She was a little dazzled by the speed of the transportation.

He opened the door for her. "My name is Jim. I'll take you out to Hangar 21."

She got in and he put her bag on the seat next to her.

It was a slow drive to the hanger because all the runways were full of traffic, airplanes, and service vehicles moving with purpose around the airport. Her driver didn't say much, as he was listening on a headset to guidance about when and where he could travel in his circuitous path to the outer extremities of the airport. Finally, they stopped at a hangar with several helicopters. The sign above the hangar door read "Hangar 21." Jim opened her door and pulled her bag off the seat, indicating she should go inside.

A female helicopter pilot came out a side door just as she entered the hangar. "I'm Captain Marica Beckman. I'll be your pilot tonight. The flight to the studio will take about twenty minutes," she said checking her watch. "I should have you there by seven-fifteen." She took Leslie's bag from Jim and headed over to a sleek helicopter sitting just outside the hangar. Tucking the bag into the backseat, the pilot waved Leslie into the front passenger seat before getting into the pilot's seat. She handed Leslie a headset before putting on her own.

As she listened to the pilot talk to the tower and request permission to takeoff, Leslie smiled. Now this was the way to beat the LAX traffic! The flight to the studio was fun as Leslie watched the snarled traffic below her. The I-405 and I-10 freeways were streams of red and white car lights from the Friday evening commute. The surface streets weren't any better. She was glad to be above it all. She laughed.

"Having a good time?" Captain Beckman asked.

"This is great!" Leslie pointed at the mostly stalled traffic below them. "I've wished to be above it all so often. I remember watching *The Jetsons* on Nickelodeon. I always wondered why we didn't all jet to work in our own personal rocket ships."

They had a good laugh at the changes that TV shows like *Star Trek* and *The Jetsons* had inspired. Flip phones. Sliding doors. Robotic sweepers. Leslie was almost sad when Captain Beckman landed at the studio.

Leslie waited until the helicopter shut down and the pilot gave her the okay to take off her headset and leave the aircraft. She could see CJ waiting for her and she was excited to thank her for getting her through the LAX mess.

"Thanks for a most excellent flight," she said as she shook Captain Beckman's hand "Awesome, really. And *way* faster than driving."

"My pleasure. Thank you for flying with Hangar 21." She handed Leslie her bag. "Glad we could give you a lift." She smirked as she said that and Leslie laughed.

Leslie turned from the helicopter...and there was CJ, right in front of her, hands on her hips, her bright brown eyes staring at her, smiling. Leslie moved as if to hug her. And stopped.

"Hey," she said a little breathlessly. "Thanks for the lift. It wasn't what I expected when you said you'd pick me up."

"Well," CJ waved at Captain Beckman, "I was going to actually drive to LAX and get you but Jerry told me to use the helicopter service they use for VIPs."

Leslie's eyes widened. "VIP? This was Jerry's idea, not yours?"

CJ grinned. "It would have been my idea if I'd thought of it. I told Jerry I was leaving the meeting to go get you and he said,

'Send the helicopter. I need you here.'" CJ mimicked Jerry's voice. "I wish it had been my idea." She reached for Leslie's hand. "I missed you."

Just then, an assistant came out a door in a large building across from the helipad. She was gesturing wildly to get CJ's attention, then beckoning CJ to come over.

CJ didn't let go of Leslie's hand. "Thanks again, Captain Marica," she said to the pilot. "Once again, you've delivered the goods." She squeezed Leslie's hand. "Come on. Jerry wants to meet you." She began pulling Leslie the toward the building.

CJ seemed excited to see her but there was something else there as well. CJ wanted to show her off to Jerry. Her hand felt good but Leslie's heart sank a bit at the prospect of being shown off like a prize dog.

"Good flight?" CJ asked her as they entered the building and headed past a guard and then down a corridor. Finally releasing Leslie's hand, she pulled a badge on a lanyard out of her pocket and handed it to her. "We'll get you a permanent one with a picture later."

Now it seemed CJ was making assumptions just like the AZM executives had done. This didn't sit well with her but she followed CJ into the conference room. She was already tired from a full day of meetings with AZM and a long flight and had hoped for a nice quiet dinner after leaving the craziness around LAX.

The room fell silent when they entered and all eyes turned to them. The walls were covered with photographs, sketches, and diagrams. A couple of the photos were of her on Astro Dome. There was a table against the wall with bottles of water, fruit, and less healthy snacks. The conference table was strewn with more photos, layouts, water bottles, and assorted wrappers.

Before Leslie could take another step, a big, beefy man of about fifty stood up and walked toward them. He had a full head of black hair just starting to go gray and a bushy beard. He offered his hand to Leslie. "Nice work!" he said. "I'm Jerry. Welcome to the team. CJ, Bonnie, and Sam—which is saying something—all speak highly of you." He laughed at his own joke.

Leslie saw Bonnie, but not Sam, at the table and nodded to her.

Jerry pulled Leslie further into the room. "Team, Leslie. Leslie," he said, gesturing, "Team." He pointed at a chair about halfway down the table and next to another open chair, then turned to one of the seated men. "I want to go over the blocking again. What have you got for me in the third scene?"

As the conversation started up again, CJ pulled Leslie to the chair Jerry had indicated and took the one next to it. Then she leaned over and whispered, "We don't need to be here long. I just wanted Jerry to see you for himself." She seemed to sense Leslie's agitation and added, "I know this isn't what you expected. It's not what I wanted either. I was hoping for some time alone with you."

The conversation at the table got more heated and then a lean man sitting on the other side of CJ and closer to Jerry leaned around CJ and said quietly, so as not to interrupt the conversation between Jerry and the scene coordinator at the front of the room, "Leslie, I'm Brad Carter, the stunt coordinator. We wanted to talk to you about some of the ways to put the principal actors into the climbing scenes. Can you work with them to get the right moves? They don't need to really climb, only look good. Kind of like what you've done with CJ, but showier?"

Leslie looked at Brad and then around the table at the expectant faces turned toward her. She knew the right answer was "Of course," but what she really wanted was time to figure out what she really wanted. She looked into CJ's pleading eyes and murmured, "Of course."

"Great," said Brad, beaming at CJ and Leslie in turn. He then turned his attention back to Jerry and the conversation at the front of the room.

Leslie pushed herself out of the chair. "I've got to go," she murmured to no one in particular.

CJ got up with her and followed her out of the room. "Leslie?"

Leslie held up a hand. "I'm still on Boston time. I'm tired and cranky and I'd like to go home." What she wanted to do was cry.

CJ nodded. "Yeah, this wasn't the greeting I wanted to give you. Come on. I'm done for the night. Let me drive you home."

Leslie's bag had been left with the guard at the door. She collected it and followed CJ to her truck.

They drove in silence for a few minutes as CJ navigated the studio streets, then out onto the surface streets and headed toward Leslie's apartment, which was within easy walking distance of Zero G. Leslie watched the bustle that was Los Angeles. Traffic had eased some, as it was after nine o'clock, but the city streets were still busy with Friday night activities.

"I'll tell Brad that you've got other commitments," CJ said after a while, "and you can't help with the principals."

"I wish people would stop telling me what I will and won't do," said Leslie, feeling frustrated. "I said I'd help and I will."

"But you don't want to."

"I didn't say that," Leslie snapped. "What I don't like is being expected to just fall in line. Everybody just seems to expect I'll want what they want."

They remained silent as they continued through the traffic-filled streets.

"What do you want?" CJ finally asked.

Leslie looked down at her hands, which were folded in her lap. "I know what I don't want. I don't want to move to Boston. It's cold there."

CJ laughed. "I hear they have nice weather sometimes," she said in a conversational tone. "And the autumn colors are amazing. They have four seasons there, you know?"

"They also have several great parks, tons of history, an okay bouldering gym and decent food." Leslie finally looked at CJ.

"I hear a *but* in there somewhere," said CJ, signaling and then changing lanes.

"It's not LA. Rent in Boston near the office is more expensive than here, if you can believe it. And it's just not *here*."

"What do you want?" CJ asked again. "I really want to know. I don't want to be one more person pushing you in a direction you don't want to go. I know what that feels like."

"I want stability. I don't care for the chaos that seems to be my life right now. There just seem to be too many paths in front of me right now. And no route to follow."

"Well, sometimes you have to build your own route," CJ said as she pulled to a stop in front of Leslie's apartment.

Leslie turned toward CJ. She reached out a tentative hand and stroked CJ's cheek. "I missed you. I missed our time in Joshua Tree. Climbing and making love with you."

CJ unfastened her seat belt and leaned over to kiss her.

"Do you want to be alone? Or can I come in?" She sounded breathless after the kiss.

Leslie was breathing heavily herself. "Please."

CJ got out of the truck and joined Leslie on the sidewalk. "Please come in or please leave you alone?"

Leslie reached for her hand and started up the walkway to her apartment. "Please spend the night with me."

CJ's phone buzzed. "Damn. Not now," she moaned.

"Ignore it."

CJ checked the display. "Shit, shit, shit."

"What is it?"

"My dad. I gotta go. Sorry. I'd really like to stay but my dad has been taken to the hospital."

Leslie took the truck's keys out of CJ's hand. "I'll drive. Which hospital?"

"Cedars-Sinai in Beverly Hills."

CHAPTER NINETEEN

Leslie drove quickly but carefully through the quiet city streets while CJ exchanged texts with her sister. It seemed that CJ's father had experienced chest pains while having dinner with a producer friend. The pains had seemed severe so they'd called an ambulance. CJ's mother and sister were already at the hospital waiting for news.

It was after eleven when Leslie pulled into the shopping center across from the hospital, finding a parking spot quickly. All the stores had closed two hours earlier and most of the people visiting the hospital had gone home too.

"Did they say where they were?" Leslie asked as they jaywalked across the street to the hospital. "This place is huge."

CJ checked her phone again. "Emergency."

Just as they made it to the other side of the street, an ambulance came down the street with lights flashing but no sound. It screeched to a halt in front of the big Emergency sign, and the driver jumped out and raced to the back to open the doors. The two paramedics pulled out the collapsible stretcher and wheeled a covered person through the big glass doors that had swooshed open at their approach.

As Leslie and CJ walked in behind them, they saw a doctor and nurse working frantically on the new patient as he was wheeled through another set of doors that said Authorized Access Only in red letters. There was an on-duty police officer standing next to the door.

CJ looked around the lobby, spotting the waiting area. A beautiful woman who looked about forty and someone nearer CJ's age, both jumped up. They group-hugged.

"Any news?" CJ asked.

"None," said the older woman, stepping back but continuing to hold CJ's hand.

Leslie hung back, not wanting to intrude, but CJ turned and motioned her forward. "Mom, this is my friend, Leslie. Leslie, this is my mom, Carol Broadmore, and my sister, Cheryl Schnelling."

Carol reached out to shake Leslie's hand. "So nice to meet you." She gave her daughter an inquiring look.

"Leslie is teaching me how to climb for the film I'm working on," CJ told her. "What's up with Dad? What happened? He's only fifty-two. It can't be his heart, can it?"

"We don't know. We were having dinner with Eddie and his wife, and he just kind of fell over clutching his chest." Carol groped in her purse for a tissue. "We thought he was joking around. You know your father. He recovered a little before the paramedics got there but I wasn't having his stories. I saw his face. He wasn't joking."

"We got here a little over an hour ago," said Cheryl. "Mom called and I picked her up. They wouldn't let her ride in the ambulance. I think they beat us here by about ten minutes. The place is a three-ring circus. We've seen two other ambulances drive in since we got here. Mom's just finished filling out the paperwork for Dad."

Carol blew her nose and tucked the tissue in a pocket. "Let's talk about something else. We can't do anything but worry until the doctor comes out."

Cheryl turned to CJ. "You're looking tan and fit. Last time I saw you, you were looking like a ghost. Do we have Leslie to thank for this?" She gave Leslie a speculative look.

"We did some filming out in Joshua Tree National Park," said CJ, looking blandly at her sister.

Realizing she wasn't going to get anything out of CJ, Cheryl turned to Leslie. "You coach climbing? How exciting. Are you going to work on the film with CJ?"

Noticing Leslie's look of consternation, CJ jumped in. "She's considering it. Working on the film. But she's got a lot of irons in the fire."

"Such as?"

"Cheryl," CJ said. "Don't push." Turning to Leslie, she added, "Don't mind my sister. She always wants to know everyone's business."

Cheryl was looking like she was going to ask another pointed question when a doctor came out. After speaking with the check-in nurse, she turned toward them and headed over.

"Mrs. Broadmore, I'm Dr. Nightly. Your husband is fine. He had an acid reflux event."

"Heartburn?" Cheryl asked.

"Serious heartburn," said Dr. Nightly. "It's not your run-of-the-mill, take-an-antacid kind of heartburn. He may have gastroesophageal reflux disease. Mrs. Broadmore—"

"Call me Carol, please. These are my daughters, CJ and Cheryl," she added, gesturing at each them. "And Leslie, a friend of the family," she finished, smiling at Leslie.

The doctor nodded. "Carol, has your husband experienced any heartburn events prior to this episode?"

"He eats antacids like they're candy. I've warned him to see a doctor but he just waves me off."

"Well, he's not going to be able wave you off anymore. This is potentially serious and could lead to other conditions if left untreated. I've already informed him of this."

"Can he go home tonight?" Cheryl asked.

"No. We want to run some more tests in the morning to ensure our diagnosis is correct. We've got him hooked up to a couple of machines to monitor his heart. Mrs. Broadmore, Carol, if you'd like to come back with me and see him…I can't let the rest of you back there, as we have a couple of very serious cases right now. I suggest you go home and come back tomorrow during regular visiting hours. He'll have been assigned a room by then."

"Thank you, Doctor." Carol turned to CJ and Leslie. "You two go home. I know you're both tired. Leslie, it was a pleasure meeting you. I hope CJ brings you by the house."

CJ started to protest.

"If anything pops up, I'll call," said Carol, reassuring her daughter. "Cheryl, I'll be back in a few minutes, then you can take me home. I'm feeling relieved and mad at the same time. This is so like your father."

After CJ and her mom exchanged a hug, CJ turned to Leslie. "How about we try this ride home one more time?"

Cheryl's eyebrows went up but she kept her comments to herself.

CHAPTER TWENTY

The street was full of cars when CJ pulled up in front of Leslie's apartment.

"I park at the gym when it gets this bad," Leslie told her. "It's around the block but I have a parking sticker."

CJ was starting to head for the gym when a car suddenly pulled out. She immediately pulled into the vacated space. The streetlights illuminated the street but it was still dim in the cab of the truck, changing only as passing car lights lit up the interior. She turned to Leslie. "It's been a long day. I'd like to come in, but if you're too tired, I'll understand."

Leslie sighed. "It's been a long day for you as well. Are you okay? With your dad and everything? Do you need to check in with your mom?"

"No. Mom meant what she said. She'll call if there's a problem. And Cheryl will stay with her tonight."

They were both silent with their thoughts until CJ reached over and laid one hand on Leslie's. "I know you've got a lot going on and a lot of decisions to make. I don't want to create additional stress for you. I know I paid you already for your coaching. What you may not have known or understood is that when Bonnie and Sam came out, the game changed. The studio needs your personal details. You've got a check coming your way."

"AZM wants a decision by Wednesday." Leslie sounded as exhausted as she felt. "Before Thanksgiving. Uhh, can we go in and talk a little? I'd like to know more about what the film wants from me and for how long. I'm not very good at short-term work. It makes me antsy for what comes next."

"Sure," CJ said. "We're both tired. Maybe this is a better conversation for tomorrow? How about we just sleep tonight?" She squeezed the hand she was holding. "I'm happy to just hold you. I'd really like to hold you tonight."

Leslie woke up the next morning to find CJ watching her. She was curled on her side with the blankets pulled practically over her head with only her eyes and nose exposed. When she opened her eyes, she could see CJ, exposed to the waist, a quilt covering her hips and lower body, leaning on an elbow and gazing at her. The early morning light from the window shone down on her mussed crown of hair and made her body glow.

Leslie could feel the answering heat in her body as she met CJ's eyes. Untangling herself from the covers, she reached for CJ. The air outside the covers was cool but CJ's skin was warm and inviting. They moved together, turning and twisting, reaching and caressing, enjoying each other. At last, Leslie pulled CJ closer so CJ's head was resting easily on her shoulder. She pulled the quilt up to keep out the morning chill.

"You have the most beautiful quilts," CJ murmured, tracing the intricate quilting on the colorful pattern of triangles and squares. "I noticed them in the camper as well."

"My mom makes them," Leslie said, running a finger along CJ's shoulder. "She loves to quilt. I get one every Christmas. It makes my dad happy because that's one less in their house." She chuckled.

"What?"

"I never really thought of it that way before but I'm sure it's true. I really love them but if this keeps up, I'll be in trouble. I'll be buried in quilts!"

"If you keep up your caresses, we won't be getting out of bed anytime soon." CJ groped for her watch, which she had put on the nightstand. "Crap. It's eight-forty! I have to be at the studio by ten."

"So…we have some time." Leslie moved one hand down to CJ's breast.

CJ rolled away from her. "I need breakfast and you wanted to talk."

"Spoilsport," Leslie said without heat as she climbed out of the warm, inviting bed. "Beat you to the shower," she called over her shoulder as she headed for the small bathroom off her bedroom.

Leslie was prepping ingredients for smoothies when CJ entered the kitchen, dressed but still toweling her hair dry. The kitchen was small but bright and cheerful with a window to the street, a small table and three chairs sitting against one wall, a picture of Leslie with an older couple hanging on the wall beside a photo of Leslie climbing at Hidden Valley on a rock formation CJ recognized from their time in Joshua Tree.

"What do you like?" Leslie pointed at fresh bananas, frozen strawberries, blueberries, chia seeds, a cashew yogurt and other assorted ingredients.

"It all looks good. I'll have what you're having."

Leslie started adding yogurt and chia seeds to the blender, pulsing it on and off as she added ingredients. The grinding of the blender was loud in the small space.

During a lull, CJ asked, "Don't your neighbors complain about the noise?"

"Sometimes. But they have some loud moments too and this doesn't last long. The noise from the streets is usually louder." As if to accent Leslie's point, a jackhammer started up somewhere outside. "It's after eight, so we usually all just play nice."

Leslie poured the thick, creamy, slightly blue mixture into two tall ceramic to-go cups. "Tell me about the film and what Jerry is going to want from me. And how long will it last?"

CJ took a sip of her smoothie. "I'm not completely sure what Jerry's going to want. At first, I thought it was just your expertise but now I think he may have you be an actor in this production. I'm still waiting to see the script rewrites." She took another sip. "This is really good."

Leslie looked surprised. "Acting? I'm not an actor."

"It would be a bit part, I think, nothing major, just a few lines." She sat down at Leslie's kitchen table. "I think he really wants to see more of your climbing. I'm surprised, too. I thought he'd just use you as a double for Susan Elliot and maybe some for Brendon Lewis, as well, depending. He was really impressed.

"The filming will be about three months with some possible go backs. Jerry has already said that he wants you on set as consultant for the duration." CJ got up to pace. "He hates to wait for anything, especially when he has a question. He's been annoyed with the delays already, not having you around and me not being the expert that Brad said I was." CJ raised her hand to stop Leslie from commenting. "Sorry, sorry, that's on me not on you. No stress. Like AZM, I need to know. If you don't want to do this, I'll call Jacob. Or you or Tom can recommend someone else...It's just that...Jerry is enamored with you."

"Sounds interesting and fun," said Leslie, leaning against the counter. "But what then? I'm out of work in three months."

CJ perked up. "Not necessarily. I've been thinking about that. I can't guarantee anything but if I get good street cred for the work on this film, I may be able to start my own stunt team. Or at least become part of Brad's stunt team. I hear he's on the outs with Jack and Jill. You could be a part of my team. It doesn't have real stability, of course...not the real stability of a nine-to-five job, but there's a lot of work out there right now."

Leslie registered that CJ was offering her a job, but all she really heard was *doesn't have real stability*.

CJ couldn't take the silence. "What are you thinking?"

"I want to help you. I'd like to do the film...It's just so different from anything I've ever done. I've always taken the path of least resistance and most security." She put her still half-full glass in the fridge. "This doesn't sound very secure."

"Not hungry?" CJ took another sip of her smoothie. "This is really good."

"Stress," Leslie said. "It makes some people hungry and makes others not so much. Maybe I'll borrow some of your dad's antacids."

"Oh, my dad!" CJ exclaimed, slapping her forehead. "How could I have forgotten my dad?" She reached for her phone and checked for texts. Not seeing any, she quickly dialed her mother.

"Mom? News?" She wandered out of the kitchen and into the small living room, back to the bedroom, and back to the kitchen, making a slow circuit of the small apartment.

At the same time, Leslie busied herself putting away ingredients, washing the blender, and cleaning up the counters. There wasn't much cleanup required. She checked her own phone for messages. One from Tom asking if she was going to be at the gym today. Two from Mia at AZM checking in on her. She looked up from her phone as CJ reentered the room.

"No issues," CJ said, answering her unspoken questions. "They'll be discharging Dad today and want him to rest at home for a few days. He's to see his personal physician but it's just a really bad case of heartburn." She sighed. "Both Mom and the doctor gave him a raft of shit. It sounds like there's exercise in his future."

"What is your mom going to do? Start walking him like a dog?" Leslie said with a laugh.

"I wouldn't put it past her. He can be so infuriating."

"Do you need to go see him? Today?"

CJ shook her head. "Not today. Mom wants to get him settled and I usually rile him up. Regardless, I need to go to the set." She put her phone in her back pocket. "Do you want to come with me? I don't want to push but I'm on a tighter clock than AZM." She paused, looking at her hands, then looking up into Leslie's eyes. "I want you to work with me, but I want you with me, too. I'll understand if you need to go to Boston. I won't like it, but I'll understand."

Leslie could feel the tug on her heart. She knew she was falling for CJ, but there was still a lot of fear in her. "Let's go to the studio and see what's needed from me," she said, making her voice sound as normal as she could. "I'll help you out. I still have a few days before I need to commit to AZM…so let's see if I can take some calculated risks."

CHAPTER TWENTY-ONE

The set was buzzing when they got to the studio. The noise from hammers, drilling, gear being moved around, and conversations was almost deafening. There were fewer people in the conference room, mostly clustered in groups of three and four and looking at diagrams or moving photos and notes around as if to sequence them. One woman took notes and wrote comments on three-by-five cards, which were added to the wall.

One of the clusters included Brad. He noticed Leslie and CJ standing at the door and waved them over and pointed at a photograph on the wall. "Jerry wants to use this climb in the opening credits as a setup to the next section," he said. He sat in a nearby chair and stretched out his long, jeans-clad legs. "Jerry also wants to reframe a couple of the clips to get the angle and timeframe he wants to capture. Leslie, he wants you to be the climber. As yourself." His expression was smug, as if he knew things no one else knew. "I understand you came in second in Nationals a few years back?"

CJ hadn't known that and Leslie hadn't said anything, but it did explain why she was such a magnificent "amateur" climber. She wasn't an amateur.

"I haven't climbed professionally in years," said Leslie, not looking at CJ. "It wasn't a good time for me."

"Jerry's daughter is a huge fan of climbing," Brad told her. "And she remembered you. She said you should have won the competition but you seemed to falter at the last minute. She thinks you threw the competition."

"I just didn't have it that day," said Leslie, showing no emotion. "If you're looking for that professional, you'll have to look elsewhere. I'm not her." She started to turn toward the door.

"Wait, I'm not calling your integrity into question," Brad said. "I just wanted you to know you have a fan in Jerry's daughter. Can I ask why you quit the circuit?"

Leslie studied him as if trying to gauge his motive for asking. "I love climbing and I hate competing. Climbing isn't about competition. It's about community and solving problems together, making yourself better. When you add money and politics to the game, you contaminate the whole thing." She paused and looked him in the eye. "Or at least, that's how it was for me. There were…are…a lot of great climbers who climb for the love of it and compete. But not me."

"Well, we will be paying you to climb," Brad replied with a touch of irony. "But it's not a competition. You, and possibly Jacob, will be the only expert climbers. Unless you and CJ decide we need additional support." He quirked an eyebrow at CJ. "Will you climb for the film?"

Leslie studied him for a long minute. Then she smiled. "I never minded getting paid to climb, only the competition. And it wasn't usually the competition from other climbers but from the tension that the sponsors tried to create. Got to have drama."

When CJ and Brad both gave her puzzled looks, she added, "Competition. Don't get me wrong. Climbers like to one-up each other but it's for fun and bragging rights. For the sponsors, though, it's all about the money and making them look good.

They bring out the worst in some people. That takes a lot of fun out of any win. So at Nationals, it wasn't about the climbing but the spectacle." She shrugged. "Kind of like the news. No one cares about the truth, only what sells. Sorry," she added, "that's my cynical side coming out."

They spent the morning and early afternoon going over the planning for the revised credit shoot. Leslie had some ideas on how they could position the cameras for maximum advantage, if they were willing to either build some additional scaffolding or move all of the equipment up a back trail and onto an adjoining rock formation. It also depended on what they could get the Park Service to agree to with regard to access.

She also spent a lot of time talking about safety. Safety and responsibility for the environment would be key for the Park Service and for the film in general. "Climbing looks fun and easy," she explained. "And it is…until it isn't. Climbing in a gym is very controlled. You can get hurt but nobody is going to die. But that's not true of climbing outside on real rocks. A minor fall can cause serious damage. A major fall can kill you. Not managing around the climb can hurt others as well if a rock is dislodged from above. Your film may not want the actors in helmets, but for the good of the kids who watch this film, you should really consider it. And anyone not shown but working near the climb should be wearing head protection."

Brad looked thoughtful. "Okay, I'll talk to Jerry about it. You make good points. And the crew, if anyone is within ten feet of the climb, will have hardhats or helmets." He turned to CJ. "And we'll work with your suggestion of maintaining catwalks near any of the more environmentally fragile areas. And limiting the number of crew." He smiled. "Although if we limit food services too much, the crew will riot. And rope off other areas that aren't needed." He laughed. "I don't want to turn around and see my crew climbing on the rocks like a bunch of wannabe climbers."

CJ nodded. "I think if we put that in the request for access, the Park Service may look more favorably upon our request. There may be areas where what we request might not work fully, but if they know we understand their concerns and are doing our best to keep things within bounds, it could go a long way." She checked her notes. "We may also want to contact the Access Fund."

As Leslie nodded, Brad said, "What's that?"

"The Access Fund is a not-for-profit, 501(c)3 rock climbing advocacy group," CJ told him. "They strive to maintain and keep open climbing areas and promote ethical, responsible climbing. And the conservation of climbing areas, too. The group is a certified land trust. They can, and have, bought climbing areas. They're advocates for climbing and most importantly...to us, anyway...they have Memorandums of Understanding with the National Park Service." CJ looked up from the notes she was reading. "If we can get that memorandum and maybe get the Access Fund's blessing," she said, "that might pave the way more easily than us creating a proposal of our own to the Park Service."

"Excellent." Brad clapped his hands once and stood. "I'm hungry. And I'm sick of junk food. How about dinner?"

"You buying?" CJ asked, also standing. "Leslie? You up for a real meal?"

It was late when they finally left the restaurant after a three-hour dinner. Leslie was the only sober one. She had spent the night nursing one beer while CJ and Brad had polished off two bottles of expensive wine. She was glad she wasn't paying the bill. The bar tab was probably half a month's rent.

Was she ready for this world of entertainment, she asked herself as they crossed the parking lot. Was this the same drama and money crazy environment she left behind with competitive climbing? She cursed the fact that Jerry's daughter followed climbing and had seen her Nationals' performance, as she had hoped to keep that stuff buried both in her own mind and from those in her current life. Buried along with her relationship with Claire-Marie. It wasn't only that Marie (she had always called her Marie) had wanted her to travel, but it had been that Marie couldn't make the grade on the professional circuit. Yes, she had competed, but she never placed higher than about twentieth in

US competition. Mid-tier. Marie had always resented Leslie and her success. It wasn't just for the money that she missed the last crux move at the National finals. She did it for love...or what she thought was love. And then, when she got back to the hotel, there was Marie with one of the premiere male circuit climbers.

Leslie shook her head. It had taken her many months and innumerable good crying jags to realize that she hadn't missed that last move for Claire-Marie. She didn't want it enough. And she didn't like the life. She hated those screaming audiences. Yes, Marie pushed her, but she was truly tired of the life. What had once been fun had turned competitive and mean-spirited. It wasn't true across the board; she knew lots of climbers who kept the spirit of climbing alive, but those that got caught up in their own hype? Well, they made it too hard to be around the sport.

Claire-Marie's betrayal was just one more symptom of a life Leslie wanted nothing to do with anymore. Was that influence of possible love happening again? CJ seemed sincere. How much was chemistry between them and how much was CJ's own need to fulfill her goal of having her own company? Was Leslie just a step on that path?

Leslie wasn't a prude. She drank, but sparingly. Alcohol interfered with climbing, as far as she was concerned. She'd seen what it had done to some of the climbers on the circuit. A near fatal crash by a drunken climbing friend had cured her of any thought of drinking and driving. It was fun to party but not to excess and not when others' lives could be at stake. This was the second time she'd seen CJ drunk in the last two weeks. That didn't make her an alcoholic, but it did give Leslie pause.

Now she needed to get home and she wasn't letting either Brad or CJ drive. CJ had followed Brad's silver convertible to the restaurant, which had valet parking. Now that they were leaving, how was she going to handle two vehicles and two inebriated people?

The valet captain noticed the problem immediately. He walked up to Brad. "Hi, Mr. Carter, nice night. Ben will drive you home. He's bringing the car around now." He waved to a blond young man with fine features who nodded and took off at a run. Leslie wondered if he was an aspiring actor with a night job parking cars. The valet captain next turned to Leslie and CJ. "Will you be driving Ms. Broadmore home?" he inquired.

His intel must be choice, Leslie thought. She nodded, and with another wave he sent another, equally handsome, dark-haired young man after CJ's pickup.

Leslie was glad that the restaurant employees knew their patrons and took good care of them. She was sure the first young man's time would get charged to Brad's bill, but it was good business, regardless. She looked at CJ, who was trying to look less drunk than she was. Brad was trying, too, and they were laughing at each other. "Do you want me to drop you at home?"

"I can drive," CJ said, her words slurring only a little.

"Not chancing it." Leslie took the driver's side as the truck drew up alongside them, right behind Brad's silver convertible. She smiled. "Looks like both you and Brad have drivers for the evening."

"Night, Brad," CJ called over her shoulder as Ben guided an inebriated Brad to the passenger seat of his car. He had drunk most of the second bottle himself.

Brad waved at both women. "No work tomorrow. It's Sunday, you know, and Jerry's being generous at this point in the production."

CJ waved her acknowledgment of the good news and Leslie called, "Thanks again for dinner, Brad. See you Monday."

Turning back to Leslie, CJ said honestly, "You're right. I do need a ride. I had a little too much to drink, it's been a long week with my dad and trying to get this job. Excuses, but true. Can I spend another night with you? It's closer than my place, which is in the canyon."

"You mentioned wanting to see your parents tomorrow. Are they in Laurel Canyon as well?"

"In the hills. I'm in a townhome off Laurel Canyon Boulevard." Leslie didn't respond as CJ got in the truck and adjusted her seat belt. "Look," she said a little sharply, "I know I drank too much tonight. You're not the only one with a lot on their mind."

Leslie ducked her head and looked away. "You're right. We're both tired. You're a little drunk and I'm not drunk enough." She shrugged. "That just means I get to drive your fancy truck again. Get in. We're blocking traffic."

The valet captain gave her a grateful look. There were two cars behind them and another pair of diners had stopped to listen to their conversation.

CJ climbed into the passenger seat, muttering as she fastened her seat belt, "Let's not give people something to gossip about."

Leslie took the left out of the parking lot and headed back to her apartment. CJ seemed to make note of her turn because she sighed, leaned back in the seat and closed her eyes.

Leslie's mind was on CJ's last comment about gossips. CJ's parents were important people in Hollywood. She was right, Leslie had no idea all the pressures CJ was under with her dad being sick and trying to make an impact in the stunt world. They both had major stressors in their lives. They just dealt with them differently.

"I'd carry you if I could, but I'm not that strong. Unless you want me to try a fireman's carry. I've always wanted to do that, but I hear it can be uncomfortable for the carry-ee." She smiled at the made-up word as she shook CJ gently awake.

CJ shook her head as if trying to wake up. "No...no, I think I'm happy to walk on my own. But thanks for the offer." She unfastened her seat belt and climbed out of the truck.

They were a little awkward as they entered Leslie's apartment. On the previous night, it had been so late that CJ had just borrowed a T-shirt to sleep in and they had just fallen into bed.

Tonight, there was much between them.

Leslie didn't know what was going on with herself, or with CJ either. The day had been fun and exciting, with Brad and CJ really interested in her perspective and her ideas. They'd asked interesting questions and had talked about problems she'd never even thought of. It was like moving an army with the final objective being the filming. A lot of people, time, and material went into a film. She was glad that her focus was solely on climbing.

But tonight had reminded her of what she had run from five years ago with Nationals. She could have gone to the international competition with her second-place finish but she had chosen to let it go and return to college for her computer science degree. At the time, it had seemed the better, more rational approach, letting climbing take second place—both literally and figuratively—to just earning a living.

Sid had let her basically create her dream job with the time to climb on the side. Now Mediasoft was being sold and AZM wanted only the product, not the process. It was the process, the problem solving, that she loved. And now CJ was offering her the problem solving and climbing, but not the longevity she craved and an uncertain future. And the possibility of the limelight. Was she ready for complications?

CJ followed her into the apartment.

"What are you thinking about? Are you still angry with me for drinking with Brad?"

"No, I'm not angry. I'm just not a big drinker."

"You can't believe everything you hear about Hollywood's drug and alcohol culture. We have our share of health nuts." CJ moved into the tiny living room and sat on the couch.

"Okay." Leslie wasn't sure where this was going or what had brought this sudden need for information.

"Are you a vegetarian?"

Leslie was surprised by the question. "Mostly. I still eat eggs and cheese. So yes vegetarian, but not vegan."

"Well," said CJ, leaning her head back, "I'm a carnivore. I don't plan on changing that."

Leslie shrugged. "Okay."

"I sometimes drink too much, but I'm not an alcoholic." She looked Leslie in the eye. "I know that's something you'll have to judge for yourself. Hollywood's a crazy place, and if you go to some of the parties, you'll definitely see that craziness. I don't do drugs unless they're prescribed by my doctor."

"Okay." Leslie sat in the old, beat-up leather easy chair that wouldn't have looked out of place in an eighties sitcom. "Why are you telling me all this?"

"Because I saw that you were unhappy at the restaurant and I don't want my drinking tonight to sour the deal," sighed CJ. "We have a connection. We jumped into bed but we don't know each other."

Leslie nodded, her eyes fixed on CJ's face now, and gripped the armrests like she was getting ready to be interrogated. "What do you want to know?"

"Who hurt you?"

Leslie looked away.

"If you're not ready to talk about it…that's okay." CJ's hand traced the stitches on a quilt made of pieces of fabric in bright primary colors. "What's your favorite color?"

"Green," Leslie said absently, turning her head and watching CJ trace the pattern with her small, neat hands. She took a deep breath and continued. "You heard Brad talking about Nationals. It was several years ago. Another climber and I were together. I was good, Marie was less so. I got all the fame, which I didn't care for. She wanted the fame and couldn't get it. I thought we were in love…until I found her with another climber—a guy—the day I came in second. That's when I left the circuit. I think she's still following the money and the trickle-down fame." She paused and took another deep breath. Her mind always shied away from the thought of Claire-Marie—beautiful, vivacious, vicious.

"I had a second relationship in college. I thought it was for keeps. We were young and so sure of ourselves. I thought we'd settle down in LA and setup housekeeping with lots of security and stability. Sharon. Well, Sharon wanted to travel and climb. She craved the excitement and the adventure. She knew about Nationals and thought it gave her an in with other climbers. She used my contacts to get a job with a climbing equipment company. It seems like relationships via climbing have never worked out well for me." Leslie looked away.

"Well, maybe we can break that cycle. I've had my own share of troubles with relationships, you know. I was so attracted to you and I wasn't sure you were gay." She chuckled. "Tom was so funny. And I don't think Sally will ever let me live it down."

They shared a laugh, which broke the tension a little.

CJ sat up straighter. "Tomorrow I need to go see my parents and check in on my house. Plants do need water occasionally, I'm told. Join me?"

"I promised Tom I'd help with a birthday party tomorrow," Leslie said. "It's my payment for foisting Jack and Jill on Joe. So go. Enjoy your family."

"More like listen to Mom poke at Dad, and Dad poke at me," CJ mumbled. Then she brightened. "What are you doing for Thanksgiving?"

"I was thinking of driving out to Solvang to see my parents, but they're going to Napa with friends," Leslie said, shaking her head. "I'm not all that good at making it up there, so they've taken to making alternative plans."

"Join me…or should I say save me?" CJ now had her hands clasped prayerfully. "If you're there, maybe my family won't snipe at me about my career choices."

"Snipe at you? I…I don't know."

CJ jumped up and paced the short length of Leslie's living room. Leslie watched. Even in the small space, CJ's movements were quick and confident.

Abruptly CJ turned back. "Please come with me. My family is important to me, even if they drive me nuts. And I want them to meet you."

Leslie sighed, "What should I bring? And don't say nothing. I can't come empty handed."

"Bring a main dish for yourself," CJ told her. "I'll warn my parents that you're vegetarian." She put up a hand. "Don't worry. Their friends have so many weird food habits they won't bat an eye. More importantly, they won't try to feed you things you don't eat."

Leslie tilted her head. "Like what?"

"Don't get me wrong," CJ assured her. "There will be tons of food, but like I said, they're used to people with strange diets. One of my mom's friends only drinks kale smoothies, which she brings with her. Reminds me of a character in a J. K. Rowling book. I've always wondered if there's anything *special* in that drink."

Leslie chuckled. "Maybe some Polyjuice Potion?"

"I wouldn't put it past her."

Leslie stifled a yawn. "Enough of this. Let's get some sleep. It'll be hard work dreaming up what kind of peanut butter and jelly sandwich I'll be bringing to your parents' house."

CJ started to protest and then she yawned too, practically cracking her jaw. "I like peanut butter. Okay, bed it is."

CHAPTER TWENTY-TWO

Leslie woke early and slipped out of bed. After putting some frozen muffins in the oven, she spent a few minutes reading her emails. She found a reply to one of her Gunks inquiries. There was a women's climbing group that sounded promising. She clicked on their website and started reading about the local activities.

A few minutes later, the aroma of muffins brought CJ into the kitchen. "I thought you said you didn't cook much." She put her arms around Leslie. "It smells good in here. What are you reading?"

"Just following the instructions," Leslie said, closing the laptop and leaning in to her for a kiss before moving to the oven. "I can reheat with the best of them. I'd normally just have a bowl of cereal but having company...I'm pulling out all of the stops. When are you expected at home?"

"Shortly. Mom's an earlier riser and I want to arrive before she can create her list of things for me to do this week." CJ reached around Leslie to snag a hot muffin from the pan as

Leslie pulled it from the oven. "Hot!" she cried out, juggling the muffin from hand to hand.

"Well, duh!"

CJ took a small bite. "Yum, blueberry...my favorite." She put the rest of her muffin on the paper towel Leslie handed her and blew on her hand where the hot blueberry had stung her.

Leslie rolled her eyes. CJ was a lot more impetuous than she was, that was for sure. If they continued to work together, Leslie would have to be the cautious one in the team. That was an interesting thought—team... That indicated longevity... As what? Friends, partners, lovers? Did she want to team up with CJ, or was it just a pipe dream as Boston was still her most likely future?

"Hate to eat and run," CJ said as she polished off a second muffin, "but you don't know about my mom's lists." She leaned over to kiss Leslie.

"Will I see you tonight?"

"Probably not. I think Mom mentioned some party or something. Although you'd think with my dad's health problem right now, they'd cancel. It's no wonder he eats antacids like M&Ms."

And, Leslie thought, if you don't slow down, you'll be just like him.

CJ jumped up from the table and collected the few items she had brought with her. "I'll see you at the studio on Monday. We need to get your paperwork in order, regardless of your choice. I think you've got a decent check coming your way already." She turned toward Leslie again. She looked like she wanted to say something, but all she did was say, "Thanks for breakfast." She looked into her brown eyes. "Good luck with your day." Giving Leslie a final kiss, she headed out the door.

Leslie stared after CJ, a whirlwind of energy and confidence. Leslie could still feel the heat of the kiss. She brushed a hand over her lips.

She had some time before she needed to be at Zero G to help Tom. Maybe a little bouldering time might help her think more clearly. She headed for the shower to get her own day started.

The noise in the Zero G gym was at a decibel level that could rival a heavy metal rock concert. The speakers were pumping out a steady stream of eighties rock music and the twelve ten-year-old kids at the birthday party were screaming as if they were watching a horror flick. She had been peacefully bouldering for about half an hour when the party started. Even though she had agreed to take Joe's place for making him deal with Jack, she couldn't help but regret her promise. There was nothing quiet or peaceful about a kid's birthday party.

Leslie wished she could wear earplugs, but she actually had to listen to the little monsters. The kids were fun to watch, though, and enormously excited to be on the rock wall. Every hold made was a chance for celebration, with yelling and fist bumps all around, and every fall came with equally loud groans and screams of dismay. The kids were having a blast. It wasn't surprising.

Leslie knew Tom would get a few future climbers out of the mix today. That was the reason he had these parties in the gym. While the one-off parties brought in cash, the potential for return climbers that paid monthly dues and the additional coaching they would need were the real money-makers.

As the kids ran off to eat cake and get an additional sugar boost they didn't need, he joined her, coiling ropes in an attempt to tidy the area. "Any potential?" he asked.

"Some." She nodded toward a girl in a green tank top that said *It Isn't Easy Being Green*. "She's really good. I don't think this is her first time climbing. The kid in the blue shirt is good, too. He has an affinity for the routes."

"I saw you bouldering when I came in to handle the party," he said. "Need some quiet time?"

"Yeah."

"Any decisions?" he asked, pushing one of the route tags back down where it had peeled up from too many climbing shoe hits.

"I can't decide if I should go to Boston." Leslie continued down the wall, managing ropes and checking the grigris, the gym-approved belay device that was used for all special events.

"Why? Not that I want you to go, but it seems perfect for you. A chance to pay off your debts and get paid real money for what you're doing. And you'll still get to climb, though, well, maybe not as frequently, and The Gunks is a world-class climbing area."

Leslie toed a pile of chalk on the mat where a kid had spilled his chalk bag. "I don't want to be a cog in a corporate wheel," she said in a quiet voice, "told what to do and how to do it. Oh, I'll get to be creative, maybe…but I won't be a part of the whole. I'll just get to work one piece of the puzzle. That's not me! I'd go crazy and bite someone's head off. Or quit. And it's cold in Boston. I hate the cold."

"You like Joshua Tree in the winter."

"It's a dry cold," she said and they both laughed.

"Does AZM know that?"

She glanced at him as the kids started singing "Happy Birthday." "Nope."

He waved his hand in an "and?" motion.

"I'll call them soon. Maybe they'll give me some more time." She sighed. "Did I mention I don't like drama?"

Tom just laughed. "Is the Pope Catholic? What are you going to tell them?"

She looked up at him.

He pushed. "What do you want to tell them?"

She picked up discarded chalk bags. "I'd like it to just go away, actually, without me saying a word, but I know that won't happen. I'll probably tell them I just don't want to move to Boston because it's too cold."

"That's lame and that's not the real reason," he said, leaning against the climbing wall.

"It's part of it. The part I like most about my job with Sid and Mediasoft is problem-solving, figuring out the best plan and route, building the site and then working with the client to improve it. AZM just wants me to build websites in a vacuum.

I'll be bad at it. It won't last." She headed toward the counter, taking the chalk bags she had collected with her.

Tom followed her. "So what are you going to do instead? You can work here full time if you want. The pay isn't that great unless, of course, you get paid what you're worth for coaching. That means you have to advertise your creds."

Leslie rubbed her face and grimaced. "I wouldn't mind coaching. But I don't want to advertise my second place at Nationals."

"It's an Olympic sport now," he said. "There'll be plenty of parents who want their kid to be the next Lynn Hill or Kyra Condie. A lot of the kids come from Colorado or New York, you know. LA could use a winner. You could be that coach."

"It wasn't an Olympic sport when I got second."

"Nobody cares about that. Only that you were nationally ranked." He picked up a climbing magazine and shuffled through the pages, pointing to the climbing coach membership and certification classes. "You need to formalize your certification. Your street creds will get you the first clients. Winning will bring you money."

Leslie shook her head. *So it's back to fame and money. Or is it? It might be fun to coach an Olympic champion.* "It's not going to happen, Tom, just not going to happen. Fame and money are why I stopped climbing professionally. Why would I do it for coaching?" She shook her head again to clear the visions of a student she coached with an Olympic gold medal. "I'd rather climb than coach. And I'm not going to climb competitively. Nice thought, but no."

"Just a thought," he muttered. "I could use the money."

Leslie patted him on the back and smiled. "You could always have Carrie or Karen coach. They might not have the creds but they're great teachers. They actually like kids. And they know climbing." She turned to go back into the climbing area. "Plus, CJ offered me a job on the film for the next three months, maybe four. That will give me time to figure things out." She decided not to mention her unsure feelings for CJ or CJ's future business plan. Her feelings were her own and she didn't know if

CJ wanted her business plan to be common knowledge or kept private.

"Well, I guess that means you won't be helping me out with birthday parties for a while."

Leslie's relief was obvious. "Guess that's what it means. But cheer up! I can still do some route setting and individual coaching, time permitting." *If I don't move to Boston.*

CHAPTER TWENTY-THREE

As Leslie drove into the studio the next day in her beat-up Chevy, she felt like a fraud, even though her name was on the list at the front gate and her driver's license got her through the gate and onto the set, where an assistant met her and took her over to security to get a permanent badge and then to accounting to fill in some paperwork. She had just been handed her check for the work with Bonnie and Sam when CJ spotted her and jogged over to meet her.

"Badged up and ready to go, I see," CJ said, noting the ID badge. "I see your picture's ready for the next NCIS mugshot review."

Leslie snorted at the joke, then waved the check at CJ. "Nice work if you can get it."

They walked into the big warehouse that housed the *On the Edge* set, which was filled with echoing pockets of noise. Conversations and hammers blended in a weird but somehow pleasant harmony.

"Nice, huh?" They headed over to where construction was going on for the green-screen climb scene.

Using Bonnie and Sam's work, the set design team had built a replica of a ten-foot-by-ten-foot section of the Astro Dome rock formation in Joshua Tree. The shape and texture looked real enough, but as Leslie studied it, she felt that something was off.

"Coloring's wrong," she said as she stared up at the textured wall.

"Now you sound like Sam," CJ said, looking at Leslie with surprise. "He said the same thing."

Leslie noticed CJ watching her. A weird expression on her face. "What?"

"You don't know how beautiful you are, do you?" Leslie scoffed but CJ continued, "You have such expressive eyes, yeah, your hair needs a trim but the style suits you. Check out that Wonder Woman pose."

"You're buttering me up," Leslie said, relaxing her unconscious pose.

"I'm not, but I know you don't want the spotlight."

CJ continued to watch her and Leslie could tell from the look in her eyes that she wanted to know her decision. "I'll help you with the film," Leslie said.

CJ looked like she wanted to jump up and down but just gave a quick fist pump.

"But," Leslie continued, "I still have to deal with AZM and Mia. What they are offering me is really good. Maybe they'll cut me some slack on the timeline."

That part took some of the wind out of CJ's sails and she dropped her hand.

"How's your dad?" Leslie asked after a short pause. "Surviving your mom's wrath?"

"Mom was really worried. I think that's hitting Dad. He might even mend his ways...for a while, anyway."

"Did you tell them I'm coming for Thanksgiving?"

CJ hesitated before answering. "Yes...well, they know someone is coming with me."

Leslie quirked an eyebrow at her.

CJ shrugged. "I told them I was bringing someone to dinner. I knew I wanted to ask you to go with me." She wasn't looking at Leslie. "I just hadn't gotten my nerve up to ask you yet so I didn't mention your name. Okay?"

Leslie kept looking at her, a question in her eyes.

CJ didn't say anything else.

"Okay," murmured Leslie.

CJ nodded. "Let me show you what they're doing for The Ivory Tower," she said, turning to head farther into the cavernous warehouse.

The day was full of consultations and reviews of sets being constructed. CJ and Leslie had lunch with Bonnie and Sam and discussed lighting options. Sam, with his favorite topic being discussed, was almost loquacious. The afternoon was filled with more meetings with Brad and then later with Jerry and the rest of the creative team. By seven that evening the whole team was tired and they were all starting to snap at each other. By nine o'clock two people had to be separated before it turned into a fistfight. Jerry called it a day. He seemed to be well pleased with the day's progress.

"My place or yours?" CJ asked, trying to stifle a yawn. "Yours is closer to the studio so we can sleep later. Mine has a hot tub if you want to relax from the tensions of the day. And my place has a little less traffic noise." Hoping that Leslie would be up for a little company, she had packed a bag. They were starting to get to know one another better, and she wanted that to continue.

"Lady's choice," said Leslie with a note of anticipation.

They ended up heading to Leslie's apartment. CJ was tired, but watching Leslie all day had made her want to have a lovely finish to what had turned out to be an excellent day. She had assured Jerry that Leslie was onboard. He'd grinned like the Cheshire Cat. She'd wanted to question that smile but had been pulled away into another conversation about climbing gear.

Leslie had parked at Zero G so CJ picked her up and drove them back to Leslie's place. Traffic was lighter at ten p.m. A couple was out walking their dog that looked like a cross between a corgi and a beagle. CJ wanted a dog so badly but her schedule just didn't give her any time at home. She wouldn't be so cruel as to have a fur friend that she couldn't keep with her.

"I want a dog," Leslie said wistfully, as if reading CJ thoughts.

"What kind would you want?"

"A husky."

CJ nodded thoughtfully. "Beautiful dogs. I'd want a border collie or a corgi, but only if I could take it to work with me. I can't abide people who have dogs and just lock them in a kennel or a small backyard all day."

"Yeah, that's why I haven't gotten a dog." Leslie unlocked the apartment door. "Can't take them on the JT trails either." She pushed open the door and flipped on the lights. "I'd be good with a cat or two but I travel too much. I'd love one of those cats who loves to travel, but again, cats aren't allowed on the trails." She dropped her backpack on the floor as CJ came in with her own small bag.

"Come here, beautiful." CJ turned and held out her arms. "I've wanted to kiss you all day."

Leslie stepped into CJ's arms, her head angled down to kiss her. Their lips were soft and warm, and as the kiss deepened, it seemed that its heat melded them together. It was going to be an interesting, exciting night.

The next two days were more of the same. Meetings and consults all day long, afternoon meetings reaching late into the night. There was friction between some of the groups but that just made the end product better as they worked scene by scene and shot by shot. Brendon and Susan came by for a short time to see the progress and to do some wardrobe checks. On Wednesday night, Jerry finally called a halt at seven p.m.

"Enjoy the weekend!" Jerry's assistant, Sheila, called out. "See you on set Monday. First location filming will start on

December eleventh." There was a collective groan. "Yes," she said, "I know it's earlier than expected. Bring your A-game next week. We only get one week in Joshua Tree National Park, so make sure you read all the briefing material. If you break any… ANY…of the rules, you will be fined. First fine is bad, second fine is worse, third fine…off the film, no exceptions." She stared hard at the assembled crew, most of whom were trying to look like they weren't ready to bolt for the door and the Thanksgiving weekend. "Not everybody is going on location," Sheila added, "so check the call sheets." She gave them one last stare. "Happy Thanksgiving."

The team broke for the door, jostling each other and calling out last-minute good wishes as they raced to the parking lots.

Before CJ and Leslie could make a break for it, however, Sheila called them back. "Wait, you two. Jerry wants a word with you both." She pointed them toward Jerry's small conference room across the hall from the main conference room.

In the center stood the round table Jerry called his desk. It held stacks of paper, photos, and a notebook computer. The walls had pin-ups of all the principal actors, the location shots and a fifty-five-inch TV screen that practically swamped one wall. Jerry was sitting with his feet up, remote in hand, watching Bonnie's footage from Joshua Tree with the sound off. As they came into the room, he paused the replay and pointed at two chairs across from him.

"Brad may have already mentioned this to you," he said, rolling the remote in his hand. "Leslie, while we're in Joshua Tree, you'll be the principal climber. Brendon and Susan will only be on location for two of the seven days. For the other five, you will be the principal actor."

He pressed play on the remote. The scene showed Leslie moving with great precision across the face of the north Astro Dome wall. The lighting was great, as the scene had been shot at one in the afternoon. It was also very intense, which took some of the beautiful rock detail away. They all watched as Leslie made a particularly hard move. She was stretched out in a spread-eagle against the rock before she finally moved one foot and precisely placed her toe on what looked like a featureless point. Then she moved up easily.

"We need to catch this in better light," Jerry said, hitting pause again. "Based on the diagrams, I think sunrise is when this would be best." He looked at Leslie for confirmation.

She nodded.

"You'll not only be the principal," he continued, "but you'll also be our chief climbing consultant. You heard Sheila's warning. You see anything amiss, you tell Sheila. She'll handle it. Don't try to handle it yourself. Get Sheila. The Access Fund and the Park Service will be there, but I want us to self-police. Read over the briefing material one more time." He turned to CJ. "I know you had a hand in writing it, CJ, but I don't want any mistakes and I don't want anyone getting hurt. It will be a big enough pain if we have to bring in a new crew member if someone violates the rules three times. But no one gets hurt." He snorted. "We could only finagle one week in Joshua Tree. It's high season there. I just hope it doesn't rain."

He looked back at the paused frame of Leslie on the rock face. "Go have a good Thanksgiving, you two. Come back rested and ready to work."

They wished him a great Thanksgiving, accepted the briefing materials Sheila handed them, and headed out.

"I have to sleep at my parents' house tonight," CJ said. "Tradition and all that." She sighed. "I'd ignore tradition, but Mom is kinda weird right now and Dad is tiptoeing around her. My brother's coming in from somewhere back east. My sister gets off because she has family. Besides, they're only two houses down from our parents." She rolled her eyes. "You'd think we were Greek. Here's the address."

"What time do you want me to be at your parents' house tomorrow?" Leslie asked, taking the slip of paper from CJ.

"I'd like you there at six o'clock in the morning, but dinner isn't until two in the afternoon. So maybe one? No later than one thirty."

"Do they know about us?"

"They will after tomorrow because I probably won't be able to keep my hands off you. Don't worry, I'll keep it PG. There are parents in the house, after all."

CHAPTER TWENTY-FOUR

At one-fifteen on Thanksgiving afternoon, Leslie pulled her Chevy, which was making a loud grinding sound, into the circular driveway at the top of Laurel Canyon. The road up had been narrow and twisty and she had made a wrong turn that had forced her to back up because the road was too constricted to turn around.

CJ was standing outside when she pulled up. "Thank God you're here! Dad is hiding, Mom is drinking, my sister is trying to get her kids to play a game outside but they want to play video games, her husband is watching the football game, and my brother is, well, my brother. Can I drink, or will that put you off? No, don't answer that." As soon as Leslie was out of the car, CJ had her in a bear hug.

"Sounds like a normal family," Leslie said as she returned the hug. "And, yes, you can drink if you're not driving. I plan to drink, too, but I'll probably only have one unless it gets really bad in there. So I can always drive you home."

CJ squeezed her harder. "Thanks." She leaned back and then in again to give her a warm kiss. "Happy Thanksgiving." She looked at the house. "You ready for this? My dad and brother may give you the third degree." She took Leslie's hand. "I promised not to get involved."

"You're such a chicken." Leslie grinned and pulled out a filled ceramic bowl from her passenger seat.

"Cluck, cluck," CJ said as she pulled Leslie through the front door and took the bowl. "Does this need refrigeration or heat?" When Leslie shook her head, she set it on a table just inside the door. "Let's go for the drinks," she said. "Maybe nobody will notice us and we can just go sit by the pool."

As soon as they got to the bar, however, a tall, lean man with thick blond hair spotted them and headed over. He was wearing black slacks and a sleek designer T-shirt that hugged his torso. "I'm Jason Broadmore," he said, extending one hand to Leslie. "CJ's older and wiser brother."

"Leslie McAllister, I work with CJ." She shook the outstretched hand. "Nice to meet you."

"Let me get you a drink." He slipped behind the bar, set his own drink down and looked at her.

"A beer," she said as she stepped to the bar. "Something dark if you have it."

"Dad usually has a pretty good selection of beer." He pulled out several bottles and she selected one. He popped the top and handed her the frosty beer, picked up his own drink and toasted her. "Just a working relationship?"

"No, we're sleeping together," she said, noting the surprise on his face. "I don't consider that work."

As Jason almost spilled his drink, CJ laughed. "You deserved that. I'll take a beer, too." She nodded at what Leslie was drinking.

After getting CJ her beer, Jason looked at Leslie more speculatively. "Where did you two meet?"

CJ looked like she wanted to say something but Leslie answered his question. "Zero G," she said easily. When Jason looked puzzled, she explained, "It's a climbing gym in the city. CJ asked for some coaching. I'm a good coach."

"Oh, that stunt 'crap' you're always on about," Jason said dismissively to his sister. "Climbing is cool, though. Isn't it an Olympic sport now?"

"For doing crap work,'" Leslie said, "CJ is doing well. She's assisting Brad Carter in stunt coordination."

Jason tilted his head and stared at his sister. "Have you now? Assistant to the great man. No more swinging from the rafters?"

Just then CJ's father walked in, looking sharp in a navy turtleneck and crisp navy trousers. Leslie thought he looked like an older, more worn version of his son. He looked a little pale from his misadventure but otherwise seemed strong and robust.

"What's this I hear about rafters?" he asked, his voice a rich baritone.

"CJ got a job as an assistant stunt coordinator with Brad Carter," his son replied.

Her dad gave CJ an appraising look. "Maybe there's hope for you. But assistant...Well, Eddie still wants you for the supporting lead in his film."

"Dad, I've already declined Eddie's offer," CJ said wearily as if she'd told him several times already.

Her dad looked like he was going start in again when Leslie stepped up. "Mr. Broadmore, I'm so pleased to meet you. I'm Leslie McAllister."

His eyes moved from his daughter and fixed on Leslie. They narrowed and then he smiled. "Call me John. It's so good to finally meet a friend of CJ's." He shook her hand warmly, looking like he was about to pull her into a hug before he stopped himself. "Carol," he called toward the room across the hall. "CJ's here. With her friend, Leslie." He still hadn't let go of Leslie's hand. "I've heard so little about you," he said. "Tell me about yourself?" Leading her over to a huge dark leather couch sandwiched between two comfortable leather chairs, he pulled her down to sit next to him.

For all that it was full of dark furniture and large built-in mahogany bookshelves, the room was brightly lit. Leslie could see beautifully framed pictures of people strategically placed around the room, though she couldn't make out details. She shot CJ a look that said *save me*, but CJ just held up her hands. Leslie diplomatically extricated her hand from Mr. Broadmore's.

She didn't know exactly who she was anymore. Most people wanted to know what you did and she was between jobs. She decided to stick with the work she was currently doing. "I'm working with CJ on *On the Edge*."

"And what is it you're doing for Jerry?" His voice sounded a little snide.

"Dad doesn't care for Jerry," CJ put in, sinking into one of the deep leather chairs and putting her feet up on a nearby ottoman. "Not since Jerry did the film Dad was so keen to get and got an Oscar nomination for it."

Mr. Broadmore scowled. "Fetching coffee and sharpening pencils for Brad?" he said to his daughter.

This sounded like an old argument and Leslie could see that CJ was going to take the bait. "Consulting," Leslie said, a little too loudly in the suddenly tension-filled room. "CJ is assisting Brad Carter on the stunt work and I'm there to give expert advice on the climbing scenes. It's fascinating work, actually." All eyes in the room were on her now. "CJ's generated some interesting action ideas and done some good location work for the film team. Jerry and Brad both appreciate the depth of what she's brought to the film." She put a special emphasis on CJ's name.

Before the conversation could go on Carol entered, carrying two bowls. She wore an apron over a chic, pale-yellow dress obviously created by a designer. CJ's sister, Cheryl, was right on her heels, wearing an equally pretty, light-blue dress and carrying a tray of cheese and crackers.

Carol set the bowl of corn chips on the large coffee table. "Are you getting excited, John? Don't make me send you back to your room. The doctor said no stress or excitement." She handed the second bowl, holding what looked like rice cakes, to her husband.

"Yuck!" He set the bowl on the coffee table and reached for a salty chip.

She smacked his hand.

"Thanksgiving," he said petulantly.

"You can enjoy your dinner," she said, "but no chips. Too much salt and oils. Do you want to have another episode?"

The room continued to fill as Cheryl's kids came in, the smallest toddling over to CJ and waving a red toy train car in a very grubby hand. "Ceeege!"

CJ stooped down and caught him up in a hug. "What have you got, J2?" Ducking nimbly as he almost bashed her in the head with the toy, she listened as he babbled at her as if it was the most interesting thing she'd ever heard. Waiting patiently at her feet was a second small child. CJ looked down. "Hi, Cynthia, how are you?"

A tiny miniature of her mother in a blue dress, the child looked at her aunt through pretty blue eyes. "Fine, Aunt CJ." To Leslie, she sounded like a six-year-old going on forty.

Cheryl set the tray she was carrying on the coffee table and smiled at Leslie. "Great to see you again...under better circumstances."

"You've met?" CJ's dad inquired perplexed.

"At the hospital, Friday night." Cheryl moved the cheese tray further away from her father's reaching hands. "Have some cheese, Leslie. The family loves this brand. It's specially brought in by one of Jason's associates."

The whole afternoon was more of the same. Jason and John continued to ply Leslie with personal questions and poke at CJ for doing stunt work when she could be a fabulous actor. Cheryl waffled between coming to Leslie and CJ's aid and making subtle jabs at CJ herself while trying to manage the kids. Cheryl's husband, unwilling to enter the fray, helped manage the kids but was otherwise silent.

Leslie did her best to deflect the questions about herself and support CJ's choices. She seemed to make a little headway but she could tell it was an old family argument. Carol did her best to steer the conversation to less stressful topics, finally telling her husband that his dinner was going to get blander if he kept winding himself up so tight. That shut him up for several minutes.

By a few minutes after two, Leslie was seated next to Jason at the beautifully set dining room table with enough silver and crystal to outshine Macy's. Leslie's Portobello Pasta Casserole, still in its ceramic bowl, was given a place of honor on the table near her. It looked a little out of place but Carol took no notice, and it was passed around with the rest of the dinner. The whole family applauded when John carried the turkey in on a huge platter, with Carol walking nervously behind him. At the table, the conversation turned to easier, more family-friendly topics and discussions of travel and friends.

Family dinners at Leslie's parents' house had always been a lot quieter, with only the three of them and maybe a few friends. None of the pomp of the Broadmores' feast and with less tension. The meal had always been basic but good with a bowl game on TV afterward.

When they were all sated with food and wine, Carol and Cheryl brought out the pumpkin, pecan, and apple pies. The group groaned but dug in and made a dent in two of the pies and polished off the pecan. Then the men and kids returned to the den to lie comatose in the comfortable chairs. Jason turned on the game so they could pretend they weren't just trying to rest and digest all the food they had eaten.

Leslie tried to go into the kitchen and help with the dishes but after she carried the dishes in from the dining room, Cheryl shooed her out, saying washing dishes was her job. She wanted to say that it was normally her job, too, but she understood Cheryl's desire to be alone for a few minutes after the drama of the afternoon. CJ helped carry the remains of the dinner into the kitchen and stayed to package up the few leftovers, such as they were. Leslie wasn't quite sure if she wanted to go back to the den where the men were watching the game.

"Let's go out by the pool," CJ said, coming up behind her. "My family tires me out, too, and I can't believe I ate that last piece of pie." She groaned as she led the way out the back to the pool area.

Leslie collapsed onto a lounge chair. "I'm stuffed. Your mom's pecan pie is to die for."

CJ joined her on an adjacent chair and they sat in contented silence for a few minutes.

"Your dad wants you to be an actor?" Leslie said. "What's he got against stunt work?"

"It's a long story." CJ lifted her face to the sun and then pointed at a hawk circling overhead. "I love Laurel Canyon. It's in the heart of the city but it still has a wild feel."

"You're stalling."

CJ sighed. "My parents sent me to acting school when I was young. My teachers said I had lots of potential. I did a few simple parts in some simple films. Like you, I hated the limelight and the attitudes of some of the actors. I didn't want to become one of them." She sighed again and rubbed her face. "Let me rephrase that. Most of the actors I know now are great folks. But as a child actor, there is so much pressure. I couldn't handle the stress. I ran away a couple of times. One time I lived in my best friend's pool house for thirty-six hours before my parents found me and brought me home. Then I stopped acting. It wasn't a good time in my life."

"But you enjoy swinging from the rafters," Leslie said, carefully watching CJ's face. "Why doesn't your dad like stuntmen?"

"Oh, he loves stuntmen, just not his daughter being one."

"He's afraid you'll get hurt?"

"Maybe. But I think it's the 'lots of potential' comment. He wants someone in the family to get an Oscar and it won't be my brother. And there aren't any Oscars for stunt work."

"Why doesn't he get his own Oscar and stop pestering you?" Leslie looked over her shoulder, checking to see that they were still alone.

"Great question. It hasn't happened yet and remember, I have potential." CJ wiggled her fingers in air quotes.

"Well, I'm not too crazy about acting in Jerry's film either. I'd rather just be in the background. Providing guidance and letting others get the acting parts."

CJ shook her head as if clearing away an errant thought.

"What are you thinking?"

"Nothing. Nothing important." CJ pushed herself off the lounge chair. "Let's get out of here and go to my place. Let's spend the rest of the weekend there. My roommate is out of town with her current squeeze."

CHAPTER TWENTY-FIVE

The rest of the weekend passed in a blur of lovemaking, hiking in Griffith Park, and a day trip climbing at Stoney Point near Chatsworth in the San Fernando Valley. The weekend ended all too soon.

As Leslie drove back to her apartment Sunday night to do laundry and check her mail, it hit her—she hadn't contacted AZM. Crap! She really didn't want to talk with anybody at AZM but she owed them an answer. Mia had been more than gracious to her. The question was whether to call tonight and leave a message or call tomorrow morning and talk with someone?

If she waited until tomorrow to call, she'd toss and turn all night thinking about it. But it was chickenshit to leave a message. The week had passed in such a blur. Boston hadn't even come up in conversation over the weekend. Why couldn't she have remembered this tomorrow instead of today? She fretted the rest of the way home, almost missing her street. As she pulled into her parking space, her Chevy sputtered to a stop. She knew she was going to have to do something about the car and soon.

Why was everything about money? The check from the studio was good money. It would pay the rent for a couple of months but it wasn't car payment money. Not yet, anyway. Maybe she should take the job in Boston. It would be steady and reliable. And if she was really honest with herself, easy.

Except for CJ.

She had yet to sign a contract with the studio for the film. They were working up a contract for her but it was taking some time due to changes Jerry wanted added. Right now, they were paying her consultant wages, which surprisingly, CJ had negotiated at a fairly high rate. CJ had also told her not to sign anything until a film industry lawyer had reviewed it. She had recommended her dad's lawyer, who she'd been going to for years. So much legal work, more money out of her pocket. After the look in CJ's eyes, she knew she needed to make sure she did get any new contract reviewed.

Grabbing her mail from the mailbox, Leslie greeted her neighbor and his dog as they went out for a walk. It was late November and her neighbor was in shorts and a light sweatshirt. Boston had been freezing. She wouldn't be surprised if they hadn't gotten snow. *Boston, and money, and lawyers…oh, my!*

As she dropped her mail on the kitchen table, one letter slipped free. It was from Mediasoft. After the news that AZM had bought them, all work was officially stopped, pending the move to Boston. She hadn't even thought about going back to the office. Expecting a final check, she ripped open the envelope.

It was her final check for work performed, but accompanying it was a letter from AZM requesting confirmation of her move and employment with them. If she did not agree to the move and the offer, her employment was terminated. As stated in her Mediasoft employment contract, no severance pay would be forthcoming if she declined the offer. There it was in black and white. Decision time.

She stared at the letter for a full minute, her mind a jumble. Dropping the letter, she grabbed her laundry and headed for the laundry room. Time to get some chores out of the way. Doing something normal and simple would give her time to figure out what she was going to say to Mia and AZM.

She hadn't made it out the door of her apartment when she was stopped by a courier with a package for her. Dropping her laundry basket, she signed the tablet he handed her and took the heavy manila envelope. It was from the *On the Edge* contracting team. Well, at least now it appeared she had some clear choices.

She pulled out her phone to text CJ.

When CJ pulled up, her pickup blocking traffic, Leslie jumped in and pulled the door shut. The truck started moving even before Leslie had her seat belt fastened.

"Got the contract?" CJ checked the rearview mirror as she maneuvered to make a left turn.

Leslie balanced the large envelope in her lap as she fastened her seat belt. "You called the lawyer? He's available?"

"Yep. His name is Sebastian Winter. He's worked with my dad for years. Everybody is always in a rush but he's willing to review it tonight. He'll be able to tell you the basics. Full review and signoff will probably take a little bit longer."

"I appreciate your help with this. I wouldn't know what to look for in a contract. I've dealt with sponsors. I should have had someone review those contracts before I signed."

"Did they screw you over?"

"Yes and no. The initial sum looked great but I basically just sold myself for a year. At least I was smart enough to put an end date on it." She looked around. "We heading back to your parents?"

"No. Sebastian lives close to my parents. Basically, around the corner."

Traffic was light as it was so late. Leslie was surprised that a lawyer would see them at nine o'clock on the Sunday night of the Thanksgiving weekend. *Yes, Hollywood is strange.*

They pulled into the driveway of a bright, cheerful house and parked behind a new BMW SUV. The house was similar to the Broadmores' place, a medium-size ranch-style house overlooking the canyon, but with scrub in front instead of the grass in front of the Broadmores' house.

Sebastian answered the door and motioned them to follow him down the hall to his office. From what Leslie could see, it was tastefully done in warm browns and big antiques. The lawyer's office was modern, with big windows through which she could see the lights of the city. Instead of being in the center of the room, the desk faced the window. What Leslie saw was a real workplace versus a showplace for visitors. The walls were covered with photographs, all signed, of Sebastian with famous people.

CJ made the introductions and Sebastian held out his hand for the contract. "Do you know what they want from you?" he asked Leslie as he pulled out the contents of the envelope.

"So far I've just been an expert climbing consultant, though I have done some on-site climbing demos for them." She took a seat in the comfortable chair he indicated. "Jerry said something about me doing some acting. I'm not too sure about that or what it entails."

"Hmm." Sebastian put his reading glasses on and started to read, then stopped and looked up. "This may take an hour or so. CJ, why don't you show Leslie the backyard."

True to his word, an hour later he called them into his office.

"It's a standard contract with a couple of extras," he said, giving Leslie a speculative look. "You continue to get an hourly consulting fee for your climbing expertise, above industry standard fee for your acting. I might add that for a non-lead, first-time performance, that's decent. And they want to use your second-place finish in the US Climbing Nationals as part of the film's advertising campaign, with promotion fees for every event you do. Minimum, twenty events, maximum, sixty. There is a small, very small, residual fee if the movie makes over two hundred million, gross." He stopped, noting the stunned look on Leslie's face. "It's a lot of money, I know."

"An ad campaign?" Her voice came out choked. "I don't want them using that in any ad campaigns."

Sebastian peered over the rim of his glasses. "It's perfectly standard. It looks like part of the reason they want you is for your record. Next year is the Olympics, so there's a good tie-in to the movie."

Leslie leaned her head back and covered her eyes with her hands.

CJ grimaced and looked at Sebastian, who was eyeing her curiously. "Long story," she told him. "Is there any way to change the contract for just that piece?"

Sebastian held up a letter that had come with the contract. "It looks like the offer is based on the ad campaign. It hints, but doesn't come right out and say it, but it looks like the assistant coordinator work you're doing is contingent on Leslie's signing as well."

"They can't do that, can they?"

CJ just nodded as if she had expected something like this.

"There might be a payout," the lawyer said, "but, yes, they can do a lot of things."

"When do they want an answer by?" CJ asked, her face carefully blank.

Sebastian looked at the letter again. "Tuesday."

"Your advice?"

"Take the contract," he said, handing it to Leslie. "It's fair. The ad campaign is only for this film. TV and promotions for one year after contract signing. I suggest whatever issue you have with promoting yourself, you get over it. This contract represents a lot of money. You must have really impressed Jerry."

They thanked Sebastian for his time and left.

"What did this consult with Sebastian cost me?" Leslie asked without much enthusiasm.

"About the cost of one of the promotion events you don't want to do."

"It's a lot of money."

"Yep."

"Crap."

They were both silent for the rest of the drive back to Leslie's apartment.

When they arrived, Leslie asked, "Coming in?"

CJ shook her head. "No. You have to figure this out on your own. What do you really want?" She reached over and caressed Leslie's cheek. "I know what my goals are and I'd like you to be a part of them. But I really just want you in my life. I don't understand all the things going on in your head, but I trust you." She wanted to add, *and I'm not Marie, either,* but she didn't.

"What about you getting kicked out if I won't play?"

"Not your problem. I'm a big girl. I'm good enough at what I do. I'll land on my feet," CJ said with a glint in her eye. She knew that regardless of what the letter said, she'd get Brad's backing. She also knew that the film really needed Leslie unless they wanted to find a new climbing expert and make more script changes, all of which would put the filming way behind schedule. She knew the reason for the sweet deal but she wasn't going to pressure Leslie. Her feelings for Leslie were way beyond what this film would mean to her career.

Leslie leaned into their caress, pulling CJ into a heated kiss which left them both breathless. "Sure you won't come up?"

CJ nodded, not saying any more than her lips had just said.

"See you tomorrow, then." Leslie watched CJ's taillights until the truck turned the corner. She felt churned up inside. The time she had spent with CJ this weekend had been wonderful. She knew she was falling in love. From the kiss they had just shared, she thought CJ felt the same. But was it Nationals all over again? She didn't see CJ leaving her for another climber, but what about for her new business?

It was late, she was tired, and she didn't think she'd be getting much sleep. She did know that regardless of what she chose, Boston wasn't even in the running anymore. It would be the simplest answer, of course, but she wasn't going to move across country to take a job that would make her miserable. *It's great to have choices.* Taking a job that would give her stability but took away a large part of the creativity wasn't an option when she had other possibilities, even if that did take her seriously out of her comfort zone.

Jerry was a sneaky bastard. Just when she was starting to have fun and be excited about the creative process and being a part of an incredible team, he'd had to pull in her past. She knew what kind of events she'd be asked to do. They'd put up a climbing wall at a premiere or they'd send her to a rock-climbing gym with studio representatives hocking the movie. Maybe even back to Nationals for a sponsorship tie-in. Back where she had started.

Am I ready to see Marie again? Am I ready to face that demon?

Marie probably had come up in the world and didn't even associate with the climbing world anymore. Leslie had always seen her as a supporting character in a successful movie, still second tier trying to make it to the top. Yes, beyond Marie, she'd enjoy seeing some of her old teammates. They might still be climbing or be coaches now. Maybe it would be cathartic to do this, and if the film was good, it could be fun. Hopefully she could put it all behind her. And she'd definitely be able to pay off a number of bills, get herself a new car…and she'd also have time to find a stable job more to her liking. All without having to move to Boston. Well, she concluded after giving it some more thought, all she had to do was deal with those demons. It was a calculated risk. If she signed the contract, she would definitely have more time with CJ. And that was worth a lot.

First thing tomorrow, Leslie needed to decline AZM's offer. Declining was closing that door and potentially letting Matt and Sid down. She knew Sid would forgive her but he wasn't going to Boston. It would be hard not working with Matt and her other friends every day but she hadn't heard yet whether they were all going, either.

Change was hard for everyone.

CHAPTER TWENTY-SIX

The drive to the Culver City studio lot was easier on the Monday after Thanksgiving. It seemed to Leslie that a lot of people were still enjoying their holiday weekend and couldn't be bothered to come into the office. She used her new badge to easily pass through the gate and parked her Chevy near the soundstage. While city traffic had been light, the set was a busy hive of activity. It looked like everyone had gotten a renewed burst of energy. Either that or they knew they had little time to get everything ready for the location shoot in two weeks.

She had called AZM before leaving for the studio. Mia had been disappointed but not surprised by her decision. "Sid said you'd be a hard sell," she'd said. Leslie had asked if many of her colleagues had chosen to move to Boston, and Mia mentioned a few names, but Matt's wasn't among them. So he had decided to go off on his own, too. She'd have to check in on him. Mia had tried to get her to reconsider by sweetening the deal a little more. Leslie had let her know about the film and the proposed time commitment and Mia said she'd talk it over with the AZM leadership team. The call ended on a friendly note. It had gone a lot better than Leslie had anticipated. She hoped her next conversation with Jerry would go as well.

Jerry was in conference with costume design when she arrived and CJ wasn't there yet. When they had talked earlier this morning, Leslie had shared the results of her AZM call and CJ had said she was thrilled that she wasn't leaving Los Angeles but she still hadn't pushed Leslie on her decision about the film. Leslie could tell CJ wanted to give her the space to make her own decisions while at the same time making it abundantly clear that she wanted Leslie near her.

Jerry had just finished with the costume designers and was heading out the door when Leslie stopped him. Sheila tried to block her but Leslie went around her, evading her out-stretched hands.

"Jerry, we need to talk," Leslie said as she stepped in front of him.

He walked around her, his long legs eating up the ground and kept on going, merely calling over his shoulder, "Got a meeting with the executive producers. We can talk when that's over." Sheila scurried after him, shaking her head at Leslie.

And, she thought, the conversation with Jerry was not going to be as easy as the one with AZM. She turned with a sigh and started to go back into the Astro Dome set area.

She almost ran straight into Brad Carter, who was standing behind her. He put his hands out to steady her but dropped them quickly as she stepped back from him. "What's up?" He pointed his chin at the door through which Jerry and Sheila had just exited.

Leslie studied him thoughtfully. "Contracts."

Brad nodded, then looked around to see how close other people were. "Let's talk." He motioned her to follow as he headed for the main conference room. They found several people in the room. He asked them to leave.

After they'd left, he closed the door and motioned Leslie into a chair. "Problem with the contract?" he asked, taking a seat two down from hers.

"I think I should discuss this with Jerry," she replied, setting her backpack on the table and watching Brad's face for signs of where this might be going.

"The ad and promotional campaign were my idea," he told her. "I'm guessing that's your issue."

"I'm not an actor."

He waved that off. "I've seen the demo reel. Some of it's you talking about climbing. You're a natural. Jerry will get even more from you."

"You're right...I don't like the ad campaign." She fiddled with a pencil she found on the table. "I'm not comfortable dealing with that part of my life."

"Maybe it's time you dealt with it."

"CJ isn't pushing for me to do this," she said, as if this was a good argument.

"CJ cares for you. Actually, I'd say she's in love with you."

Leslie stared at him, openmouthed.

"It's not my place to comment, but I've known CJ for years. You've gotten under her skin. Hell, she even took you home to meet the family."

Leslie didn't know what to think. Replaying the last few days in her mind, she felt the warmth in her chest expand. Yes, CJ had just crept into her own heart so easily. She seemed so self-contained...but Leslie wasn't sure. CJ was physically, but not verbally, demonstrative.

"Is that so much of a surprise? Like, you thought she was going for you only for what you could do for her career?" He frowned at her. "CJ isn't like that. She's been amazingly non-pushy with you. She usually just plows over people who get in her way." When Leslie didn't reply, he gazed around the room for a few seconds. "CJ called me this morning. She said she knew we needed you more than you needed us. She asked me to kill the promotional events part of the ad campaign."

Leslie looked at him silently, not quite ready to take another emotional hit.

"She might be right," Brad assured her, "but I think *you* need the promotional campaign to put some of your demons behind you." He was using the same words she'd used just last night. *Demons.* "Especially if you and she want to make a life of it."

Without another word, he got up and walked out the door, leaving her sitting alone. Her mind was reeling from all this new information. She thought of CJ's hand on her cheek last night. *How had I not felt the love?*

Her thoughts were interrupted when a group of people entered the room, noisily heading for the snack table without even noticing her. They grabbed coffees and snacks and started a review of the scene deconstruction posted on the wall, moving cards and diagrams around.

Leslie sat and watched them for a few minutes. Maybe Brad was right. CJ wasn't Marie. She had never felt for her what she felt for CJ. Marie just seemed like a bad dream. A trust broken.

Pulling her backpack toward her, she removed the contract. Taking a pen from the table, she turned to the signature page and after a brief hesitation, signed. Then she began initialing all the flagged pages. Maybe it was good that she hadn't talked with Jerry. Brad had the answers she needed, or maybe she'd find them herself, thanks to that necessary push he'd given her. Sometimes she got in her own way. She slipped the contract back in her backpack. Busy day with two big decisions made.

CJ arrived just in time to see Brad pull Leslie into the conference room. She thought about interrupting but stopped outside the door. She had promised herself she wouldn't interfere. But was stopping this conversation between Brad and Leslie interfering or was it stopping the interference? She was still pondering this when Bonnie came over with some questions.

A bit later, while she was demonstrating a climbing move, someone reached in from behind her and pushed her hips into the wall, moved her right arm slightly and turned her left hand upward. Momentarily startled, she relaxed as she recognized Leslie's sure touch.

"Hi!" CJ stepped off the wall and faced her.

"Hi." There was a smile in Leslie's voice as she pulled CJ into a firm hug. Her cheek rested on her collarbone and her body fit nicely against Leslie's.

CJ pulled back and looked into Leslie's eyes. "Well, it looks like somebody came to a decision. Did you decide you have the winning lottery tickets?"

"You might say that," Leslie said, giving her a last squeeze before releasing her.

"Did you talk to Jerry?"

"Not yet. But I have a couple good ideas about the promotional campaign."

"You've signed the contract!"

"Daring greatly, as old Teddy Roosevelt would say." Leslie mimed an old man and wiggled her eyebrows.

CJ laughed, then quickly sobered. "Are you ready to do this? It's actually really hard work. And the money slips through your fingers faster than you'd expect if you aren't extremely careful."

"Do I need a money manager?"

CJ shrugged. "Some people do, though you seem to be fairly frugal. Just don't go crazy and you should be okay."

"I don't know the plan for how I'll be paid but I'd just like to pay off some student debt and get a reliable car. The Chevy's about done."

"Well, first you have to earn it." CJ towed Leslie over to where Bonnie was talking with Sam.

CHAPTER TWENTY-SEVEN

The next two weeks were extremely hectic with costume design and fabrication, script changes, and gear checks. Leslie's whole life changed because now she was the one getting fitted for costumes and being asked to learn lines. This completely freaked her out until CJ gave her some tips one night while they were cuddling.

"Look, you know climbing. Understanding the scene is over half the battle. The dialogue should seem to come organically from what is happening. What you're doing. Read the script over again, understand the story, work up your lines in blocks and then work through the lines with another actor to get context and rhythm. I'll help you if you like."

Leslie levered herself up on one elbow. "Would you? I don't have a whole lot of dialogue. The climbing is the easy part. I feel like I sound really wooden...like I'm a big fraud." She caressed CJ's hair and then pulled her in for a kiss. "I appreciate you so much...Geez...that didn't come out right." She snorted in exasperation. "And you wonder why I try not to talk too much."

Rolling over on her back, she put her hands over her face. "Brad said something to me the other day." She paused, then plunged ahead. "I think I'm falling in love with you...Is it too soon? Am I crazy? Should I get a U-Haul?" She lifted a hand and peered at CJ. "I'm kidding about the U-Haul. Though since we've been spending so much time at my place, you might as well move in for the duration of the film. Oh, geez, I'm still talking when I should be listening. Please say something."

CJ sat up and turned to face Leslie. "I think I'm falling in love with you, too. I'm scared, though."

"Of what?"

"Of you. Of me. I'm the daughter of a director and a producer."

"And people have tried to use you to get to your father and mother."

"Yep."

"Well, that sucks."

"How is it that you can make me laugh when I want to feel sorry for myself?"

"It's either laugh or cry. Crying gives you puffy eyes, laughing gives you wrinkles. It's a toss-up."

"You should give up acting and do stand-up." CJ gave her a playful shove, which she deftly avoided.

"Fat chance. This acting gig is a one-time shot. I need to find a real job once this film is done and the ad campaign is over."

"I did offer you a job working with me, you know. If I can make it work..."

"Let's hold that thought. You need to work on trust. And me? Well, I need to work on getting through the next few months of too much attention." Her tone turned sarcastic. "And you don't know how much *I love it*."

CHAPTER TWENTY-EIGHT

It felt a little like déjà vu as Leslie drove Tom's camper into the Hidden Valley campground. She even managed to get the same campsite, which was something of a miracle, given the time of year and the climbing population. There had been a big rainstorm the night before that had cleared out a number of less hardy campers, but today the sky was clear and blue.

She had been offered a room in town with the rest of the crew but had declined. She liked being in Joshua Tree and feeling its calming influences. The park gave her balance and settled her in a way no other place did. She knew this trip would be different from her last trip. Before she had been a guide and now she would be an actor in a film. Too weird. But feeling weird was for another day. Today she was just going to get settled in and do some bouldering.

CJ would join her soon. She had needed to get some additional gear that was a last-minute add, so she would arrive at the camp later in the day. Jacob would also join them. He wouldn't be staying with them in the camper, of course, but would take an adjacent campsite with some climbing friends. His own fan boys, as it were, he had laughingly told her on the phone.

It was chilly when Leslie set up. She had arrived early so she'd have a full day of climbing before filming started tomorrow. Tomorrow it wouldn't just be her guiding another person or a small group. A lot would depend on her, the safety of multiple people, and in some way, the whole look and feel of the movie. She'd had several discussions with Jerry about what he was trying to bring to the film. It was more than the acting and the plot: it was the essence of Joshua Tree. Joshua Tree needed to come alive as if it was a living, breathing entity. It was the lead and the people supporting actors. Sam had seen this in the texture, colors, and spirit of the rock.

While she waited for everyone to arrive, she decided to work with the rock and find her own balance with the park. She finished her setup quickly and pulled her crash pad, shoes, and chalk bag from the camper. Then she set out to build confidence and find a calm space within herself.

Later that morning, CJ met her on the trail as she was coming back into camp. CJ's hug lifted her off the ground.

"I'm happy to see you, too," Leslie said when she had solid ground under her feet again. "Glad to see me or glad to be back in JT?"

"To see you, of course, but I also have great memories from our time here," CJ said with a wide smile. "My dad called before I left. He actually wished me luck…well, luck in his own way." She struck a pose and spoke in a respectable imitation of her father's voice. "Have fun and don't kill anyone."

"That's good luck?" Leslie's eyebrows lifted.

"From my dad, that's the 'Hallelujah Chorus.' I think Jerry talked to him about my work. Settled him down a bit, though I expect this won't keep him from harping at me about not acting."

"Anything from your mom?"

"She asked about you and where I was staying," CJ said with a smirk. "I think she likes you."

"Your mother's high opinion of me matters. Did you see Jacob?"

"And his team of rowdies, too. Luis is back but no Freddie. I think there are five of them. I didn't catch all their names."

"Everything's ready for the setup tomorrow?"

"It will be tight. We only have two days to set everything up. *And* there's what Jerry added last night." She sounded exasperated. "We're short on crew, as we have to limit our footprint here. The rain didn't help. And there are new restrictions from the Access Fund. With the rains, they have some additional precautions we need to take. We could ignore them, though. They aren't in the contract. However, Jerry and the location manager are adamant that we keep the locals happy."

They had reached the campsite. CJ pulled some papers out of her backpack and handed them to Leslie. "These are the updates."

Leslie looked up from the notes. "Nothing major. They just want us to stay on the trails and watch out for the water." She noticed how intently CJ was watching her. "What?"

"Wanna fool around while we still have the energy?"

Just then, they heard Jacob's booming voice. "Hey, there's the star!" He walked around the other side of the RV.

Leslie looked helplessly at CJ and she shrugged.

CJ's phone alarm woke them at five a.m. They had stayed up late sharing stories with Jacob and his friends and Leslie had brought them all up to speed on expectations. Two of Jacob's friends were with the Access Fund and would be monitors on the film crew. They were all really excited about showcasing Joshua Tree but not too sure they trusted the crew to keep to the agreements.

Hearing the alarm, Leslie sat up and groaned. After some randy sex with CJ last night, her mind had gone into a continuous loop of the tasks she needed to deal with at Ivory Tower. There were going to be two teams, one setting up on Ivory Tower, the other at the north face of Astro Dome. She would be the expert in charge and Jacob and Sam would be responsible for location two and setting up for the Astro Dome shoot. It felt like she had just fallen asleep when CJ's phone began ringing insistently.

"Come on, sunshine," CJ called as she leaped out of their shared bed and raced to the bathroom. "First day on location is always my favorite. Complete, organized chaos."

Leslie groaned again and fell back on the bed. Maybe she could get another few minutes of sleep while CJ was in the bathroom. No. She needed coffee, then breakfast, and then to make sure Jacob was up, and then…lists of tasks were already racing through her head. She stumbled out of bed and headed for the coffeemaker.

The location was buzzing when they arrived. Large trucks and trailers with bathrooms, dressing rooms, and makeup rooms lined Park Boulevard near the Key's Corner parking area. The sun wasn't even up yet but bright lights illuminated the area and riggers were calling to one another as boards were placed to facilitate the movement of scaffolding, trollies, and gear. There was a cheerfulness to the crew's banter as they readily insulted each other. They worked as a team, moving fast and methodically, as if laying track for a train.

Leslie's only job for a while was to watch and ensure that all of the guidelines and rules were followed. One of Jacob's Access Fund friends was there, too, with two park rangers to make sure the team members knew where they were going. The sun was starting to peek over the horizon when the food service truck arrived to great fanfare. There was a great deal of jockeying for position for coffee and pastries before work resumed with a vengeance.

By lunchtime, half of the trucks had been driven away to be stored outside the park until the pathway would be pulled up at the end of the location shoot. The boards, six-feet wide and ten-feet long, had been laid out in a continuous pathway for the crew and actors to use all along the trail. Lines were also strung along the path of boards for the riggers to stay between as they brought in additional structures and gear. Scaffolding was being erected quickly and efficiently, rising forty feet into the sky. The team was going faster than Leslie had imagined. CJ, moving between locations, said they were right on schedule.

"So far, so good," Leslie said. "Sheila must have put the fear of God into them."

"The riggers get a bonus if there are no mistakes and it's on schedule," CJ said as she watched the work progress. "Woe to the rigger who screws up."

"Must be a hefty bonus."

"Twenty percent. Since the location schedule has been compressed to a week and there's a limited number of people, there's money for incentives to do it right the first time." CJ stepped aside as another group of riggers hustled by with the long scaffolding stanchions.

"How's it going at Astro Dome?"

"Slower. It's farther to the formation. They're about a day behind this group. But filming starts here. You're on tomorrow, then Brendon and Susan for two days with you coaching, then back to you. Last day is teardown."

"That's a change. I thought I was up after Brendon and Susan, not before." Leslie could feel the fear creeping into her voice. "I'm not ready."

CJ shook her head. "Sorry, that was mean. I know how stressed you are, but I had to get you back from scaring me with Route 499 my first climbing day in JT."

Leslie rolled her eyes and made a tick mark in the air signaling that she had fallen for the dig and CJ had scored a point.

"They're up first, although you may have a couple of lines. Stop worrying. First day is all climbing, or rather, mostly climbing. I think you have two lines. Todd will be here later this afternoon with the final script for tomorrow."

Just then two riggers stumbled in front of them, one tripping over a raised board. It seemed like they were going to go off the board path when another rigger came from behind, blocked his fall and caught the poles. CJ and Leslie clapped in appreciation.

"I give that a ten!" exclaimed CJ. "Riggers are amazing. It's too bad I didn't catch that on film for the crew outtakes."

The riggers picked up as if nothing had happened and went back to their fast, efficient pace.

By three that afternoon, scaffolding, rigging, generators, miles of electrical cabling, location lighting, basic structures, and even two port-a-johns were all in place along the basic board path. Camera lighting and camera equipment were checked then removed to be put up again in the morning. CJ seemed to get more energized as the day wore on. She made sure the specialty rigging needed for the climbing segments went in as required.

Later that afternoon, Leslie and Michael, from the Access Fund, climbed up the gully at the back of the Timbuktu formation to set the anchors for Leslie to rappel down to set the quickdraws in place. Leslie found it funny that all of the quickdraws had been painted green so they could be digitally removed. They had all agreed that the weather was good and that the quickdraws would be good for the next day.

It was late when the crew left the area. Private security would be camping and patrolling on-site to ensure that no one messed with the setup overnight. Apparently fans had been known to sneak onto a set and snitch hardware. The Park Service had also set up a patrol to check the area paid for by the studio.

Jerry hadn't been on-site yet. When Brad had asked, Sheila informed them that he was back at the studio working through last-minute details but she'd kept him up to date with all of the location information. He would be arriving early the next morning with some additional people for the start of filming.

When the film crew and riggers finally headed back to Yucca Valley, Leslie and CJ headed back to Astro Dome, the second location near the Wonderland area. Jacob and his group were just watching the last of their crew leave when Leslie and CJ pulled up in CJ's truck.

"All good?" called Leslie, joining him as they watched the parade of cars and trucks head down Park Boulevard toward the park exit.

"Climb on," said Jacob, smiling and giving the ready-to-climb tag line. "We will be done by noon tomorrow according to the location manager and set designer. They say we're doing well."

CJ joined them. "Any issues?"

"A couple of close calls," he said, "but no problems. The park staff seemed very happy."

"Excellent! Let's head back to Hidden Valley. Tomorrow's going to be a busy day."

But before CJ had taken more than a couple of steps, Jacob called to her, "Do you know a Ginger Smytheson?"

CJ dropped her head and gave a sad nod. "Why do you ask?"

"She was here with a friend. They asked a lot of questions of the film crew. Leslie's name came up a few times."

Leslie turned to CJ. "Who is she?"

"Jerry's daughter. You know, the one that ratted you out about Nationals. She's trouble. Uses her dad like a bank and he lets her." CJ turned to Jacob. "Did you catch her friend's name?"

He shook his head. "I didn't see much of her, but she looked really familiar."

"Trouble?" asked Leslie.

"I'm not sure." CJ paused and looked around. "It doesn't sound good, though. Let me check with security again."

Jacob and Leslie exchanged a look of concern as CJ strode off to talk to the Park Service and the security coordinator.

"What is this Nationals?" Jacob asked.

Leslie didn't want to talk about it, but she knew her Nationals win was going to come out soon enough. "I managed to come in second in the US Climbing Nationals a few years ago. Jerry wants to capitalize on that for the film. That's why I'm in the film as more than just a stunt double."

"Ah," Jacob said, appraising her. "I knew you were good, but I didn't realize how good."

"I got lucky."

He made a noncommittal sound, but before he could speak, CJ rejoined them, waving to the patrol as it left.

"They're going to warn the other team. It's probably nothing."

CHAPTER TWENTY-NINE

The next day began with another early morning alarm. Jolted awake, Leslie almost beaned CJ in the head. They were tangled together against the cold under the quilts.

CJ managed to move, but barely. "Hey, watch those elbows, they're lethal," she muttered in a scratchy "I'm not awake" voice.

When Leslie tried to roll over and almost got CJ again, CJ bounded out of bed and tore the covers off Leslie. "Up! Big day ahead!" Leslie squeaked and CJ laughed. Leslie made a grab for her and CJ, still laughing, headed for the bathroom.

Leslie watched CJ go. She didn't know when she had been so happy. CJ was transforming her life and now she could see a real future for them together. Smiling, she got up to dress and make coffee.

They'd have breakfast onsite. CJ was right, the food was glorious and kept everyone from getting low blood sugar, which probably prevented a lot of hunger-induced arguments. Smart of the studio to provide good and plentiful food. She was only afraid of eating too much and having to carry extra weight up the climb.

Today was Brendon and Susan's first day on location. Leslie had been coaching them at Zero G early in the mornings before the gym opened for the past several weeks. They were both capable and willing learners and she was pleased that they knew they just needed the basics and how to position themselves to best effect. They had played like children for the first few days in the bouldering cave, then worked hard with her to work on some precise moves that she had set up to emulate the moves they would be making for each of the climbing scenes. Susan had better flexibility and could make the final positions, but Brendon was better at giving the climbing the precise movement that was similar to her own style of climbing. It had been fun working with them.

Today she wondered how they would deal with the outdoor setting and the exposure on the rock at Joshua Tree. Susan had been really good on the precision work they'd choreographed for the scripted scenes but she had never scaled the wall to the top of the climb like Brendon had. That hadn't been a problem since Leslie had been working with them on short sequences. Leslie knew that being outside the controlled environment of a gym could affect people differently. Some people loved gyms and hated the outdoors and the reverse was equally true. She was glad they wouldn't be climbing Astro Dome. Susan had confided that she was afraid of heights. Ivory Towers had height but not like Astro Dome, and the exposure was not as great either.

She knew the two wouldn't really be climbing the full route. The plan was to raise them to the sections they would climb and let them do the precise movements that had been planned for them. It would look real enough but they would be anchored and supported the whole time, even though in the final cut it would look like they were free climbing without protection, unlike Leslie's climbs for the following day, which would show traditional climbing with her placing protection along the way.

After a quick breakfast on-site, Leslie and Michael headed back up to the anchor they had set the previous night. Carrying extra gear and the rope Brendon and Susan would be using, they wore their harness and climbing shoes. The climbing rope, woven of green fibers, had been procured especially for this film.

The climb up to the anchor wasn't especially difficult but Leslie and Michael took their time and spotted each other as necessary. When they arrived at the anchor, the area looked disturbed. Yesterday they had set up two three-piece equalized anchors but now two of the cams they had placed in one anchor were missing, and while the anchor was still in place, a quick pull showed it was no longer equalized.

Michael reached down and pulled on one of the cams from the second anchor and it came free readily in his hand. "What the…?"

Leslie was already on the walkie-talkie she had brought with her. "CJ? CJ, it's Leslie, we have a problem," she said, trying to keep her voice calm.

CJ's voice came back quickly if a bit crackly, "What did you find?"

"Anchors have been moved up here," Leslie said. "Have the team check everything. And warn Jacob."

"Copy. Should I come up?"

Leslie looked at Michael. He shrugged.

"No," she said into the walkie-talkie, "we've got this. Give us an hour. We're going to reset and test everything."

"Copy," said CJ. "Expedite if you can. I'll let Jerry and Brad know the situation. They just arrived with Brendon and Susan."

"We'll do our best," Leslie assured her, "but safety first." She nodded at Michael, who started on the reset.

Damn. CJ knew it was going too well. She also knew this "mishap" was Ginger's doing. Smytheson's daughter loved to cause trouble, though Jerry didn't see it. And with no proof, CJ couldn't make an accusation. Ginger wouldn't dirty her hands climbing, though. Who, CJ wondered, was the friend? She went off to find Sheila. They needed to confirm each individual on-site and make sure that no further mischief had been done. It was going to be a long day.

About forty-five minutes later, Leslie rappelled down from the new anchoring system she and Michael had set. Climbing back up, she checked and rappelled down the second anchor. They had decided that he would stay at the anchors and monitor the area to prevent any further possible disruption… if the culprit was still around. Jacob had cajoled the other two climbers in his group to help out. One of them would be joining Michael on the rock.

The rest of the day went as planned. Susan freaked out a little but seemed to get it together. She and Brendon were able to duplicate the moves they worked on so diligently in the gym with Leslie's coaching from the sidelines. Jerry, working with the director of photography, and Sam were really happy with the final results and congratulated Brendon and Susan before they left for the day.

Jerry's daughter, Ginger, showed up without the friend late in the day, but she didn't come out to the climbing area. Security had already been warned to make no exceptions to who was allowed into the filming location. Ginger had put up a fuss but for once her father didn't relent. So she was waiting as Jerry and CJ came back to the line of trucks on the road. She kissed her dad, then turned to CJ, who was heading off to talk with Brad about the next day's work.

"Hey, CJ," she called.

Reluctantly CJ came back toward her as Leslie came up the trail with Sheila. "Ginger," she said without enthusiasm.

"Aren't you going to introduce me to your friend?"

Jerry, not aware of the tension, called out to Leslie, "Leslie, come meet my daughter, Ginger."

Leslie walked up to the group. "Hello, Ginger."

"I saw the videos of you at Nationals. You were great!" Ginger gushed, reaching out to take Leslie's hand in both of hers.

Leslie could feel the caress in Ginger's hands. She extricated her own hands after a quick handshake. "Thank you," she said without expression.

Ginger turned to her father. "Daddy, I want to watch Leslie climb tomorrow. It's so exciting! My friend, Claire-Marie Kincaid, is in town. She and Leslie climbed together at Nationals. Wouldn't it be so exciting to have them climb here together?" Ginger's eyes glittered as she coaxed her father while also watching Leslie to see her reaction.

"Ginger, honey," Jerry replied, "that's sounds interesting, but we have the scene already blocked out and don't have time for changes. I know how good Ms. Kincaid is, but not for our tight filming schedule, and Susan has the lead."

Ginger looked like she was going to try again but then said winningly to her father. "I understand. But we can both watch, right?"

Happy not to have to deal with his daughter's attempt to change the film schedule or its cast, Jerry quickly turned to Sheila, "Add Ginger and her friend to the approved list." Turning back to her he said, "It's so good to have you here. Do you have a place in town? Do you want to have dinner tonight?"

While Jerry began making plans with his daughter, Leslie and CJ turned and quickly left. Hearing Claire-Marie's name had hit Leslie hard but she had managed to keep her expression unchanged.

Once they were out of earshot of the crew, CJ turned to Leslie. "Is this going to be a problem?"

"I don't know. It's been a long time and I'm in a much better place now emotionally." She caught both of CJ's hands in her own. "I have you and I feel good about my work here."

"But?"

"But I don't know how well I'll climb with Marie in the audience." Leslie turned to look at the rock formation, which was growing dimmer as the sun dipped below the horizon.

"Marie?" CJ said slowly. "Marie...*that* Marie?"

Leslie started to say something, but just nodded.

"I can tell Sheila and get her name off the list," CJ said and started to turn.

Leslie grabbed her arm. "No. You heard Jerry. She's on the list now. If we pull her off the list, Ginger will go whining to Daddy, and Jerry will want to know why his order was countermanded." She sighed and rubbed her face. "I knew she'd pop up during the promotional campaign." Another, deeper, sigh. "I'll just have to deal with it now."

CJ pulled her into a hug and rested her head on Leslie's strong shoulder. "You've got this," she murmured. "And you've got me."

Leslie's grip tightened around CJ's waist and then relaxed as CJ's words hit home. "You've got me," she repeated.

CJ and Leslie arrived at Ivory Tower early the next day. It was before dawn, so they wore headlamps that illuminated the areas not already bright from the generator-run lighting that had just been turned on in preparation for the camera setups. Michael was expected shortly and would be joining Leslie in checking the anchors. There would be no top roped climbing today, but the second camera would be using an anchor to get shots of Leslie's ascent.

Leslie was nervous. She had a few lines, which she and CJ had worked on last night. Trying to anticipate Jerry's direction for today, they had in fact worked them a couple of different ways. With the crew's limited time on location, Jerry had decided to film everything, even the run-throughs, to maximize his choices. He even had camera drones up today.

"I won't tell you to not be nervous," CJ said to Leslie. "That would be like telling water not to be wet. I will tell you that you've got this. The climbing. The lines." She took Leslie's face in her hands and stared into her eyes. "You. Have. Got. This." Then she kissed her.

"Thanks." Feeling a little breathless, Leslie rested her forehead against CJ's. "I needed that. I need you."

They both turned quickly when they heard a polite cough behind them. Jacob wiggled his eyebrows at them. They all laughed, breaking the moment, but not the feeling.

It was after seven before everything was set and climbing was ready to begin. Leslie had said her lines and posed as Jerry had indicated. It had sounded flat to her but Jerry remained cheerful. He said they'd work on it again after the climb.

She had just roped in when Ginger and Claire-Marie showed up. It was hard to miss them, as Ginger gushed at all the crew about how *amazing* everything was. Jerry rushed over to quiet his daughter and meet Claire-Marie, but Leslie's calm was shot. She could tell by the smug smiles on Ginger's and Marie's faces that this had been planned out in advance.

Claire-Marie had gotten even more beautiful over the years. Her fine features had matured and become more regal, and now her auburn hair, still glossy and luxurious, was swept back from her face. Her smoky gray eyes flashed as they met Leslie's and then turned on Jerry with warmth. Claire-Marie was dressed for climbing as if Ginger had not told her she wouldn't be climbing.

Even though Leslie couldn't hear the conversation, she knew that Ginger was once more trying to convince her father to let Claire-Marie be in the film. Leslie felt Jacob's intake of breath as he came up behind her and saw Claire-Marie.

"*Guapaaaaaa!*" he breathed.

"Yeah. Beautiful," Leslie muttered, "but look, don't touch. You could get burned." She turned to see the stunned look also on CJ's face. She wanted to go over to her but she was already roped in for the climb. She should have warned CJ but she had somehow thought CJ knew.

CHAPTER THIRTY

Ex-girlfriends, Leslie told herself, were sometimes hard to deal with, but when your ex was a beautiful, semi-famous actor…well, it went beyond hard.

Although Jerry looked like he was losing a battle, Leslie wasn't going to let him. She looked at Sam, who was watching her, and pointed to the man he was standing next to and indicated he should start rolling film. It wasn't for her to say, but Jerry wanted everything and she was going to climb. When she saw Sam nod, she elbowed Jacob, who was still gaping at Claire-Marie.

"Ready to do some belaying?" she asked, her voice quiet but sharp. "Or are you just here to look good?"

He jumped a little when she poked him but turned his attention away from the vision and nodded. "Climb on."

She quickly removed her hoodie and tossed it back and away from the rock. She took another look at CJ, the love for her solid in her eyes, then turned back to the climb. She stepped onto the rock. Her motions were precise and yet fluid. Her stops to shake out her arms from the burn were graceful, as if she were a dancer moving with the wind, not against it. Her face was serene, yet fierce in concentration. She climbed for the love of climbing and for CJ. When she moved to the final crux, the entire crew held its collective breath. Her move was a confident one, yet from the ground it looked like she would fall. Then, in a clearly defined move, she leaped for the final hold. She hung on by one hand, then casually placed her feet before she looked down at Jacob, nodding to him. It was good that there was no dialogue in this section, as the crew was roaring when as she slipped up and over the top of the rock.

She didn't want to go down immediately. She knew that her climb had been everything Jerry was looking to capture in the film. She could do it again but now she was scared. Would CJ think she was a fraud? Would Marie's presence damage the trust that she was working to build with CJ?

She heard the call on the walkie-talkie that Michael carried. Someone was asking for her. She wanted so much to ignore it, but she accepted the device. "Leslie here."

"You were inspiring," CJ said.

"That was for you."

There was a long pause before CJ said, "I know…You still have got some *splaining* to do, though. Jerry has some words for you as well but come down now. Most of the drama is over." There was another pause and the line crackled. "Ginger must have promised Claire-Marie something. She looks pissed."

As soon as Leslie's feet hit the ground, Sheila rushed over. She returned Jacob's quick fist bump before turning to Sheila.

"Wow, just wow! I think we got it in one!" Sheila sounded out of breath, as if she had done the climb instead of Leslie. She paused, smiling at Leslie, then shook herself and remembered why she was there. "Jerry wants to see you in the playback tent."

Grabbing her hoodie from one of the techs, she followed Sheila back to the tent.

Jerry's voice reached her as they entered the tent, "…see how the light hits just right as she moves, it catches her hand movement just right."

Sam nodded his agreement as they continued to watch the playback on the small screen between them. So focused were they on the screen, in fact, they seemed oblivious to her presence. They kept commenting on the climb, the light, the camera angles. It seemed that all of the cameras had been rolling, not just the one Leslie had signaled.

Sheila pushed into the tent behind her. "Jerry," she called, "here's Leslie."

Jerry turned and looked at her in amazement, "Nice! Can you repeat that on Astro Dome?" he asked, getting right to the point.

"It's multi-pitch," Leslie told him, "so it will be a little slower and probably not quite as elegant. There aren't a lot of rest spots on Astro Dome. And it's a much longer climb."

Jerry nodded. "We'll only be taking clips from the climbs, so that shouldn't matter. We can't make the film three hours long and all climbing…though your climb was a thing of beauty. So strong, yet elegant." He paused and gave her his broadest smile. "We'll still need a couple of pickups, but excellent work. Take a rest. We'll call you when we're ready to go again."

She wanted to see CJ, but there was Claire-Marie, standing right in her path. "Marie," she said. She knew Claire-Marie hated being called Marie because she felt that she had earned the respect of her full, proper name over the last few years. "Marie" had been merely what Leslie had called her when they were just young climbers on the circuit. Back then, it had been a familiar nickname. But that was years in the past.

"I go by Claire-Marie now."

"Yes, I know." Leslie started to walk around her.

Claire-Marie grabbed her arm. "Why didn't I get this film?"

"I don't know. I'm working stunts, not casting." She shook her arm free. "I didn't even know you still climbed."

"You don't have to climb to look good on film," Claire-Marie said. "You just have to have the moves…And *I have the moves*. And I look great." She came closer, angling her body toward Leslie.

Leslie stepped back. "I'm not interested in your moves." She had gotten over Marie years ago and knew Marie was putting on this performance for a bigger audience than just her. It was too public. Leslie looked around and noticed that Ginger had her phone trained on them. "Put the phone away, Ginger. The show's over."

Hearing the voices, Sheila bustled over to Ginger and demanded the phone. "Closed set. No phones."

Ginger dodged her and put her phone in her purse. "Daddy said I could have it."

"Not to take photos or video with," Sheila persisted. "Hand it over." She gave Ginger a steely look. "You might be able to hoodwink your father but I see you." She held out her hand.

Leslie walked past this conversation. Claire-Marie kept pace. "What did you promise CJ?"

Leslie stopped and turned. "You leave CJ out of this."

"Leave CJ out of what?" CJ stepped out from behind the boulder where climbing gear was being stored.

Claire-Marie turned to CJ and purred, "Leslie loves the limelight. She's a user. Once she gets what she wants, she'll leave you for greener pastures."

CJ looked at Claire-Marie, then at Leslie. "No," she said briskly. "I think I know who the user is. Leslie, Jerry needs you for the pickups."

Leslie's eyes widened with hope but CJ turned away and marched up the path to the climb.

"Go away, Marie," Leslie said as she turned to follow CJ. "And take your bile with you."

The trip back to the RV was quiet, as neither Leslie or CJ wanted to break the silence. It had been a full day with more tension than either of them had anticipated. As CJ parked her truck next to the camper, Jacob came to the passenger door.

"Leslie, can you introduce me to that beautiful creature?"

"Nope." Leslie shook her head. "And you're better off for it. She'll eat you up and leave you without even your dignity."

She climbed out of the truck and when he started to follow, she faced him and laid one hand on his forearm. "Give it a rest. She's not in my life anymore and I'm glad."

She followed CJ into the RV and as soon as the door was closed, CJ said, "Is that what she did? Ate you up and left you without your dignity?"

Leslie pulled a beer from the fridge without a word and slid into the dinette booth, putting her feet on the opposite bench. She drank down half the bottle in one go. "Pretty much," she said. She set the bottle down on the table with a thud and looked up at CJ. "I thought she was the one."

"And is she still...?" CJ asked in a quiet voice.

Leslie snorted and then laughed, "Nope." She drank the rest of her beer, then looked up at CJ again. "It was the best day of my life when I caught her in bed with that climber. It made me face the fact that she didn't love me and never would." She looked at her empty beer bottle. "Although it took me six months to figure that out. I told you about my girlfriend in college. I thought I was in love then, too." She stopped abruptly and pointed her empty bottle at the fridge. "Can I get another one of these?"

CJ, who had not moved from her position leaning against the counter, pulled two beers out of the fridge and handed one to Leslie.

"It's strange how time can blur those edges," Leslie said after taking a sip of the second beer. "Young love, I guess. So raw and emotional." She looked up to find CJ staring at her. "I didn't know what love was. I do now."

Leslie could see that CJ was really listening to her. She felt her heart responding but was she mistaken again? Was it just infatuation between them? She looked away and took a sip of her beer. She knew what her own heart was telling her. She had known for sure when CJ had looked at her before she started climbing today.

"I guess the promotional tour will be a breeze."

"Why is that?"

"I was afraid of being pulled back into the whole climbing world. The one thing Marie said that was true was that I did get addicted to the limelight. Until I didn't."

"And?"

"I'm enjoying the climbing but I don't want to be an actor any more than you do." She saluted CJ with her beer.

"The camera seems to love you," CJ said, being equally honest.

"I'm not looking to share a bed...or a life with a camera."

"What was that?"

"A life...I don't want to share my life with a camera." She sounded exasperated, but she wasn't looking at CJ. She began pushing her two bottle caps around on the table.

"And who or what do you want to share your life with?"

The RV was silent for a long moment before Leslie sat up straighter. "Do I need to call your mom to ask her for your hand in marriage?"

CJ's eyes went wide.

"What? You don't want marriage? How about living in sin with me?" Leslie got up and leaned in for a kiss. Then, angling her head a little, she pulled CJ into a deeper kiss.

A buzzing phone interrupted them, then a second buzz. CJ pulled her phone out of her back pocket. Checking the first message. Clicking on it she showed Leslie a Facebook post.

"Looks like your altercation with Claire-Marie got posted."

Leslie shrugged. "Unless it got edited there was nothing there."

CJ checked the second message. "It's from Brad. It looks like *Extra* picked up the feed and it's on the late entertainment news now, too."

"Awesome. My parents watch that show."

CJ's phone buzzed again. "Brad. Jerry can't decide if he's pissed or pleased. No publicity is bad, you know." She smirked. "I think we can be assured that neither Ginger nor Claire-Marie will be back on set tomorrow." She began to scroll through new messages coming up on her phone.

"Why do you say that?"

"Whether Jerry thinks all publicity is good or not, he's not going to interrupt his shooting schedule, not even for his daughter. The real question is whether the news media will show up."

"No bet," sighed Leslie. Could this week get any worse?

CHAPTER THIRTY-ONE

When Leslie and CJ showed up at the shoot the next day, they found two media agencies being blocked by the Park Service. Jerry had shown up before sunrise and was talking with a woman in a sleek business suit. Both voices were loud and animated. As Leslie and CJ approached, the woman walked briskly off toward the media vans.

"Morning, Jerry," CJ said, looking after the woman, who was now spotlighted by cameras.

"Cynthia will handle the media," he said by way of reply.

"Are you going to feed them or let them figure it out on their own?"

"I think we can use this as a first push for the promotion campaign," he said, leading them back toward the food service trucks. "Not the way I'd want to go about it, but you use what you're given."

Leslie bumped CJ's shoulder before she could say anything else. She could tell CJ was upset and would probably say something she'd regret. She was trying to think of something to say herself when Claire-Marie came out of one of the makeup trailers. CJ stopped dead and Leslie almost bumped into her.

"What is she doing here?" CJ asked.

Jerry's voice was smooth. "Susan isn't in the picture anymore. Seems she wasn't okay with the heights, had a bit of a nervous breakdown last night, and is currently at a private clinic. Her agent was adamant that she wouldn't be able to continue. Claire-Marie was available and can step into the role."

"Convenient," CJ muttered. Then more clearly: "I'm sorry to hear about Susan. Are you sure she's okay?"

"Yes, I think so. She wouldn't take my call. I'm really not happy, as her chemistry with Brendon was great, but we can't wait. We'll have to reshoot part of Tuesday's scene with Brendon but at least Claire-Marie can climb and isn't afraid of heights."

"How are you going to work that in with our current schedule?" CJ asked pointedly. "Astro Dome is tomorrow."

"Leslie's work yesterday put us ahead of schedule," he said, smiling at Leslie. "I've already rescheduled for Claire-Marie to shoot today. Leslie will be on Astro Dome tomorrow. Check with Sheila on the specifics." He turned and headed for the playback tent.

"You're happy about this. You think this will be good publicity for the film," CJ accused him as he walked away.

He just waved his hand over his head and continued on.

CJ turned to Leslie, who had been watching. "Are you okay with this?"

"I don't know how I feel about her being here, about climbing with her again. It brings up memories," she said, finishing the thought in her head—both good and bad. The intensity of their relationship had been a hot flash in her life, heating her up and then leaving her cold and alone. Marie had wanted so much to be famous and she didn't really care who she stepped on to get there. Still the heat. Like a moth to the flame. "It doesn't seem like I have much choice," she said aloud, trying to keep it light. She could tell CJ was angry.

"Oh, there you are!" Claire-Marie's silky voice edged out the regular noise of the crew setting up for the day.

Leslie and CJ turned as she laid her hand possessively on Leslie's forearm. She was dressed in an outfit similar to what Susan had worn the previous day, an ensemble of lightly worn climbing pants, a tight navy tank, and a tan hoodie with *Woman Power* stenciled on the front, topped off with a forest green Patagonia puffy jacket. The jacket was her own affectation against the chill of the December morning in Joshua Tree. It also set off her auburn locks. Her makeup was camera ready.

Leslie sneezed as a whiff of Claire-Marie's floral perfume hit her. She stepped back, jerking her arm free from Claire-Marie's warm hand. "I see you got your way. Again."

Claire-Marie eyed her like she was a prize already won. "Of course, I'm *that* good. I look forward to being with you...on set."

CJ snorted.

"I don't think you need my help with the climb," Leslie said in a cold voice. "Good luck. Or is that break a leg?" She needed to leave before she got really angery and said something stupid. "I gotta go find Michael and check the anchors."

"I'll leave you to it." CJ gave Leslie a last look before turning to go.

"She's right, you know," Claire-Marie called to CJ's back. "I do get what I want. And I can offer her more than you can." As CJ turned to walk away, Claire-Marie chuckled softly.

"Let it go Marie," muttered Leslie as she watched CJ's retreating back before turning her own back on Claire-Marie and heading down the trail to find Michael.

The day passed slowly. Claire-Marie did the climb better than Susan had, though CJ took solace in the fact that she wasn't in Leslie's league. There had been a lot of takes to get the right angles and lighting. CJ was sure it was because Jerry couldn't get what he thought he was going to get from Claire-Marie.

To his credit, Jerry hadn't asked Leslie to help Claire-Marie. She did know the moves and the scene. She was photogenic and a decent climber, but Jerry had seen Leslie climb, and his expectation had risen appreciably. CJ couldn't help but feel some smug satisfaction. The newcomer might be drop-dead gorgeous but she didn't have Leslie's climbing grace.

Brad and CJ worked the stunts from the ground to ensure that everyone was safe and rope management was clean. Leslie had coached them on climbing safety. Even if CJ didn't like Claire-Marie or her attitude, there wouldn't be a mishap on her watch. There had been no more "pranks" with gear, either. CJ still didn't know who had been responsible. She couldn't see Claire-Marie pulling gear any more than she could see Ginger climbing on rocks. Probably disgruntled or opportunistic climbers; the film crew had shut down a couple of very popular climbing areas. As Leslie had mentioned to her before, gear left was free gear to another climber.

Brad and CJ formed a formidable team as they worked through all the climbing stunts. He had even consulted with her on some of the other scenes he was working and had taken some of her suggestions. She wasn't going to let Claire-Marie's words get to her. It wasn't a bidding war on who could do more for Leslie.

Leslie was putting gear away from the Astro Dome set when she felt fingertips on her neck. She turned quickly and ended up with Marie's arms around her. Before she could move away, Marie brought her lips down on Leslie's. Her lips were warm and inviting and full of memories. Leslie's arms, which had reached up to push away the fingertips. somehow got locked between them and it was a moment before she could push Marie away.

"No, Marie." She wiped her sleeve across her lips as if to wipe away the kiss and the memories. "I'm not interested in a repeat of seven years ago. I got over you."

Claire-Marie stepped toward her as if she hadn't spoken. "We're so good together."

Leslie stepped back and spotted Jacob as he emerged from the next trailer over. "Hey Jacob," she called. "I've got somebody you should meet."

"¿Sí?" he replied. Then, seeing Claire-Marie, he said breathlessly, "*Tengo que llamar al cielo para avisarles de que se les ha escapado un ángel.*"

Leslie began laughing at his reverent tone as Claire-Marie looked Jacob up and down, seeing his broad shoulders, blue-black hair, and chiseled dark features.

"Once more in English," Leslie said, moving to put some gear boxes between her and Claire-Marie, while leaving Jacob a clear path to the object of his affection.

Without taking his eyes off Claire-Marie, he murmured in slightly accented English, "Gotta call heaven to tell them an angel got away." He swaggered up to her and kissed her hand.

This time Claire-Marie gave a delighted laugh.

Leslie took that moment to make her exit.

It took her a little while to find CJ, who was in the playback tent with more people than the tent should hold. They were watching the dailies of Leslie on Astro Dome. Jerry had stayed to manage Claire-Marie's climb while Sam had worked the second unit at Astro Dome.

The shoot had started a little later to let Leslie check the anchoring setup for the Ivory Tower scene. Still, the climbing was as first rate, if not as clean, as her previous days. Although there were a few missteps on the four-pitch climb, the cameras did indeed love her. Three cameras had covered the action, one long, one short, and one tight on her face. The tension in her body versus the serenity in her eyes had been captured clearly. Jacob's work had also been showcased and he was no slouch. The defined working of his muscles would definitely bring in the female crowd and probably gay men as well. The multi-pitch action also showed some of the intensity and panoramic nature of the area. The light playing on the sculptured landscape gave the climbing depth and texture.

Leslie didn't want to disturb the group. She spotted Sheila at the back of the tent and touched her shoulder. When Sheila turned, Leslie nodded toward CJ and Sheila nodded back, maneuvering through the crowd of viewers to poke CJ and point to Leslie. Brad caught the movement and turned. When he saw Leslie, he smiled and gave her a thumbs-up. Leslie smiled back at him as CJ joined her at the back of the tent.

"Can you leave now or do you have more to do tonight?" She pulled CJ out of the tent. "I'd really like to get out of here." She looked behind her.

"Let me see if Brad needs anything." CJ looked down the path to see what Leslie was worried about. "Problem?"

"Marie doesn't know the meaning of no." Leslie's frustration was clear.

CJ looked closer. "Is that lipstick? She cornered you?"

Leslie looked chagrined. "She surprised me."

"No big zing?"

Leslie wanted to lie. "I will admit she packs a powerful punch but it's heat, not love."

"Good to know," CJ said. "Give me a minute, and we'll get out of here."

It took them another hour to leave. The call sheets for the next day had to be completed. There was a new scene between Leslie and Claire-Marie that hadn't been in the original script. It required more dialogue of Leslie than she had dealt with before. Instead of a few scattered lines, now she had several pages of dialogue.

"I'll bet this is Marie's doing," she complained as she climbed up the steps into the Tom's RV. "She can't show me up climbing so she's going for the acting."

CJ followed her into the camper, taking the script updates from her. She sat down at the dinette and read the sheets quickly. "Maybe. Have you read this?" she said, waving the pages at Leslie.

"No, I just counted the pages and the number of lines I have." Leslie began pacing in the tiny space.

"You're making me dizzy," CJ said. "Stop and read this." She thrust the sheets at Leslie as she passed.

Leslie harrumphed but took the sheets and read through the script. Then she read through it again. "This isn't bad," she said, sounding surprised and looking up at CJ. "I'm not sure Marie will be happy with this. She has good lines but I have better ones, right?" She looked down at the pages again. "How do I memorize all of this by tomorrow? I'm not a trained actor." There was panic in her voice.

"I'll help you. Same plan as before."

"Why isn't this being done on the sound stage? We have such limited time in JT."

"I could speculate," CJ replied, "but I really don't know. I think Jerry knows you're comfortable here. He wants to give you and the film the best chance for success."

Leslie sighed, "It's still a lot of words."

"Then we'd better get started."

They ended up making a game of it. Almost like strip poker, as Leslie got more of the lines correct, CJ lost more clothing. That was a good thing, as Leslie didn't have anything left to take off. The game ended with the lines learned and a steamy night of sex.

CHAPTER THIRTY-TWO

The sound of the alarm was particularly jarring the next morning. They had gotten to sleep very late. CJ didn't jump out of bed with her normal morning cheer but snuggled into Leslie's back, pulling the quilt over her head.

Leslie fumbled for the phone, which was still stuck in the pocket of CJ's hoodie by the side of the bed. She turned off the alarm and was highly tempted to snuggle back into CJ's embrace. But remembering the call sheets and the day's activity wrecked any thought of sleep, and she crawled out of bed.

"Up and at 'em," she said sweetly as she dragged the covers off CJ. "You don't want to miss my Academy Award-winning performance, do you?"

CJ yelped as the covers left her body. It was cold in the RV, the temperature having plummeted overnight. She glared at Leslie, rolled out of bed, and grabbed her clothes as she headed for the small bathroom, mumbling something under her breath that Leslie couldn't catch.

"Do I want to know what you said?"

The bathroom door shut with a definite click.

Leslie wasn't as calm as she was pretending to be. Climbing was straightforward and fun. There was a pattern and a rhythm to it. Acting was…well, hard. Today was her last day of acting. Unless there were some unscheduled pickups, her part on camera would be complete. She would continue to help CJ and Brad with all things climbing. She just had to survive the day. A day of on-camera acting with Marie.

CJ dropped Leslie off at makeup before heading over to see Brad. She knew there was gear that needed to be located and packed and studio work had to be coordinated.

Brad was at the catering truck munching on a breakfast burrito and waving a cup of coffee as he talked with the head rigger when she found him. Noticing her, he called out, "Hey, CJ, did I mention how happy I am that you found Leslie? Jerry was still raving about the dailies from yesterday. Not to mention the day before."

CJ merely smiled. "What's on your agenda for today? I'd really like to watch Leslie's performance."

"Jerry wants to talk about the next action sequences. I thought you'd want to participate. You had some good ideas and this is your chance to make a pitch on a different type of stunt, show your versatility."

"I know I should meet with Jerry, but I really want to be there to support Leslie. I put this together and I want to see it come together. Can you push the Jerry conversation off until later?"

"Okay, but Jerry's time is limited."

She was torn. She really needed to watch this critical scene. She wanted to be there for Leslie.

Brad was watching her and she felt she should justify her statement again but before she could say anything more, he said, "But yeah, she's going up against Claire-Marie." He nodded. "I saw the call sheet updates." He took another bite of his burrito. "I love this catering group. Go, watch your girlfriend." He smiled at CJ's surprised expression. "We can work on the car chase later."

Even with the smaller crew due to the park restrictions, there were still a lot of people congregated in a small area. What space that wasn't taken up with people was taken up with gear and what seemed like miles of cabling. All this was making Leslie more and more nervous. At least she was back in her normal climbing attire. Costuming had seen what she'd worn in the demo reel and had decided it was perfect for the film: worn, comfortable, mismatched climbing gear.

The text from Mia earlier in the day had helped as well. Seemed that AZM wanted her enough to give her the space and time to do the film and the publicity events though once the events completed, they expected her to be ready move to Boston. She'd almost wished they hadn't accepted her request. It was great to be wanted, but this reprieve felt like a fallback position, not a move forward.

She was fretting over this when Claire-Marie appeared, surrounded by her support staff. Except for the makeup artist, Leslie wasn't sure what the five people trailing her did. The makeup artist tried to get her to stop but Claire-Marie wouldn't be sidetracked. She walked with purpose toward Jerry, who was deep in conversation with Sam and Sheila. Walking right in front of him and practically pushing Sam aside, she said in a voice that would have worked well on a stage, "Are you trying to ruin me?"

The crew that had been bustling about getting ready for the early morning call froze and turned almost as one to see how Jerry would react to the interruption.

"Ms. Kincaid," Jerry said in a slow, calm voice, "I'm discussing the camera and lighting with Sam. Please finish with makeup. Our schedule is tight today and we don't want to lose the light."

Claire-Marie didn't recognize the anger behind the calm in Jerry's voice. As he turned back to Sam and Sheila, she made a grab for his arm and missed. He swung back toward her. "Ms. Kincaid, enough. Use your anger in your upcoming scene."

With his eyes still firmly on her, he called over his shoulder, "Liz, fix Ms. Kincaid's makeup for the scene."

Drama was what Marie excelled at, Leslie thought as she watched Marie stalk off with Liz, her staff trailing in her wake like strange ducklings. She knew Marie would take it out on her. She had hoped that Jacob would put Marie in a better mood but she also knew it was too much to ask, even if they did get together. Claire-Marie was there to make a point and Leslie was going to get the sharp end of it.

It was another thirty minutes before Claire-Marie showed up again and another fifteen minutes were spent checking camera angles and lighting. Most of the setup had been done with stand-ins, but the light was changing fast and last-minute changes in dialogue and two additional climbing scenes had been made to the call sheets. Finally, they were ready for the take.

Claire-Marie stalked to the face of the cliff and took the rope Brad handed her. He watched as she tied in and tested the knot. He took a second locking carabiner attached to a rope from the anchor at the top of Ivory Tower and clipped it onto her harness loop next to the figure-eight knot. He tightened the lock on the carabiner and then checked it with a firm push to ensure it was locked. It was a redundant measure that would catch her on a second belay if there was a problem. He finally nodded his approval and moved back to stand with CJ to watch the scene.

Leslie was already set up for the belay, and even though Brad had checked Claire-Marie's figure-eight, she walked over to Claire-Marie and asked in a low voice, "Are you ready for this? I can do this stunt for you." She reached out to check Claire-Marie's harness and rope connections.

Claire-Marie batted her hand away. "I'm ready and I know how to tie in. Just do your job." Her face looked pale, paleness accentuated by the makeup. It wasn't an awesome look, given her naturally warm complexion, and it pushed her facial features into stark contrasts.

Leslie nodded and moved back to tie into the ground anchor. Once it was complete, she looked to where CJ was standing with Brad. She hadn't approved of the morning's changes. It wasn't that Marie couldn't do the action as written, but it had been a long time since she had climbed regularly and Leslie didn't think this was something that Marie should even be doing. She had insisted on doing the belaying, though in the film it would be Brendon's role. Leslie wanted to stop and recheck all of the anchors and ropes but the light was where Jerry and Sam had planned and now was the time to get the shot. She took a deep settling breath, looked at Jerry and nodded.

Jerry nodded back and then called to Claire-Marie, "Ready?"

Claire-Marie nodded with a stony stare, then settled an intense look on her face.

"Action." The boards clicked and Claire-Marie, with a final look in Leslie's direction, turned and began her climb.

Leslie had walked through the scene with Jerry and Brad the day before without Claire-Marie. It was good that the dialogue came organically or this would never work.

Claire-Marie started up the climb, tentatively at first, then with growing confidence. She clipped into the waiting quickdraws, a two-carabiner combination with a strong nylon strap between them. When she had reached the height they had agreed on, she stopped clipping in and started the free climb section. Now although she was still on rope any fall would be a drop, and a more significant drop, as she continued upward.

Leslie watched and continued to let out carefully-controlled lengths of rope as Claire-Marie climbed. The crew behind her was dead silent, everyone intent on the action. Claire-Marie was forty feet above the last clip when she suddenly and without warning took a misstep. She seemed suspended for a moment before she came off the rock face and plummeted toward the ground. Leslie, who had been watching intently, was already pulling in rope before she began her downward motion.

A collective intake of breath could be heard as Claire-Marie fell, then, as the rope caught and held, a sudden exhalation. Leslie felt the fall on her own harness as the force tried to pull her off the ground, but her anchor held and she remained firmly grounded. But she wasn't paying attention to the wrench at her waist or to the crew. She only had eyes for Claire-Marie. She saw as well as heard the Velcro on the harness ripping free. Claire-Marie hadn't fastened her harness properly. The knots and carabiners were in place, but the harness was loose and Claire-Marie, after plummeting sixty feet, was now rotating as her harness gave way. Her legs were still firmly captured by the harness but the belt strap around her waist was in motion.

"Rope!" Leslie screamed, hoping that Claire-Marie could hear her over the distance and the panic in her own mind. "Rope!"

After her scream pierced the rest of the noise, things happened very quickly. Jacob rappelled rapidly down the rock face, heading for Claire-Marie. The guys assigned to the inflatable fall bag were in motion toward the cliff face. Claire-Marie grabbed the rope, stopping her rotation. Within seconds, Jacob had a firm arm around her and she had her arms around his neck. Luis started a second rappel down at a more sedate pace and between them, the two men lowered Claire-Marie to the ground as Leslie released rope from the main belay as the harness, while not completely fastened, was still attached to Marie.

The cameras kept rolling.

The medical team met the climbing group just as the two men eased Claire-Marie to the ground. Other than the expected bruises, she was uninjured, though shaken. Her harness, still loose, was still around her waist. Jerry had gotten the fall on camera—not the one planned, but one that was even more dramatic than the scripted one.

As her own shock wore off, Leslie started laughing. There was a tinge of hysteria.

CJ, who had run over to help pull the rope in when Marie began her fall, looked at Leslie with concern.

Leslie tried to stop laughing and finally choked out. "Upstaged again." People looked at her, but only CJ heard her words. "Who will see my wonderful climbing? All they'll remember is her coming off that rock and twisting in her harness." She paused to catch her breath. "I wonder if Jerry has an excellent editor to put the sequence together to work that drama?"

"So you weren't scared?" CJ asked.

"Sure I was. But for all I know, Marie did it on purpose," Leslie said. "I always checked her harness but she pushed me off. Maybe I'm giving her more credit than she deserves. It was a dumb thing to do if it was on purpose. So many things could have gone wrong."

They both watched as Claire-Marie was carried from the scene, a team of people following in her wake.

"I thought you might be still in love with her," CJ said.

"You know I would never do something like that. That was a stupid, potentially fatal move that could have put the whole film in jeopardy. She should be thrown off this set. But she won't. She always manages to come out smelling like a rose. I only hope that Brad and Jerry don't blame you for her crap."

Before CJ could reply, Sheila bustled up. "Jerry wants to know if you can still do the last climb or if Ms. Kincaid's mishap has put you off?" Turning to CJ, she added, "Brad needs you over at the command trailer."

Leslie snorted. "Tell Jerry I'll be ready when he's ready for me. Tell Sam I'll save his light."

CJ turned to her "You good?"

Leslie nodded and CJ took off to find Brad.

She decided to boulder while she waited for Jerry and the crew to get ready for the next scene. She needed calm and this was the best way to bring that calm back. She snagged a padded mat from a pile used to protect gear and moved down the path from the set. She laid the mat out near an easy problem she had seen. She cleared her mind of the day's activities and concentrated on the problem at hand. Her hands reflexively moved, opening and closing as she imagined herself on the short climb. Dipping her hands in her chalk bag one at a time, she stepped up to the climb and began.

She was five feet off the ground and climbing smoothly when CJ found her. Leslie hesitated on a move, not sure where the next foothold was to push her to the final dynamic jump to the top. When her foot slipped and then her hands gave as she popped off the wall, CJ jumped forward, hands up, and guided Leslie away from an awkward fall down to the thin mat.

As Leslie landed feet first and rolled, taking most of the force out of the fall, CJ sat down hard on her butt. Leslie turned to look at CJ sprawled next to her. "I love you," she said as she reached for her hand. "Sure you won't marry me?"

"Yes," said CJ remembering the conversation from a few days ago when Leslie asked her to marry her. "Call my mom."

EPILOGUE

The crowds were wild when Leslie and CJ pulled up in their limousine for the premiere of *On the Edge*. Leslie let CJ pull her from the car, the ring on her left hand flashing. Most of the crowd were shouting at Brendon and Claire-Marie as they walked the red carpet, and then a few people saw Leslie and yelled to her. She stopped with CJ to sign a few autographs and take a few selfies with the fans.

As they continued to the spot where Claire-Marie was extolling the film to *Extra*, *Entertainment Weekly*, and other media outlets, they saw Brendon and Jerry standing nearby, beaming and ready to take their turns in front of the microphones and the cameras.

Leslie had spent the last few months promoting the movie and Zero G had hosted the first event to decent fanfare. The gym had mostly been full of Leslie's friends from the gym, Carrie, Joe and the others. They had whooped at some of Leslie's climbing clips, critiquing her moves, but mostly just enjoyed the show.

Other gyms and venues had followed and it had been easy to talk climbing with eager teenagers and twenty-somethings. Leslie would never love the limelight, but she played along, knowing this was a limited engagement.

The two women had also had a limited engagement. Leslie had indeed asked CJ's mom for her daughter's hand in marriage. CJ's dad had been a little miffed and Cheryl and Jason had just laughed when they heard, ribbing him about it.

Their wedding date had arrived and once more they'd been back in Hidden Valley. The campsite had been filled with their friends and fellow climbers. They had teased their parents with plans to rappel down The Old Woman rock and let Tom marry them, but in the end it was just a fun celebration of the joining of their lives with good friends and family present. If the reception afterward had included bouldering, well, that was just bringing things around full circle.

Watching Claire-Marie preen in front of the camera, CJ whispered, "Ready for your next picture?"

Leslie shook her head. "No. I think I'll take that job offer I got last week." She slipped one arm around CJ's waist.

"Job offer?"

"Some guy named Brad wants me to build and maintain a website for him and this new, improved and expanded business. He said he wasn't going to discuss it with his new partner. He was making an executive call. I think he and his partner are calling it Calculated Risk, LLC."